ARCHANGEL™

FROM THE WINTER'S END CHRONICLES

ARCHANGEL™

FROM THE WINTER'S END CHRONICLES

BOOK ONE: ASCENSION

Maya Kaathryn Bohnhoff

based on a screenplay by David Di Pietro

Reel Cool Entertainment

Oxford, Georgia

PUBLISHED BY
Reel Cool Entertainment
25 Wildflower Trail,
Oxford, GA 30054

ISBN-13: 978-0-578-49461-6

Cover design: Dave Di Pietro
Interior design: Danielle McPhail,
          Sidhe na Daire Multimedia

DEDICATION

This series is dedicated to Jules Verne and H.G. Wells,
authors extraordinaire and the true fathers of science fiction.
Without their imagination and sense of wonder,
none of these wondrous worlds would have been possible.

CONTENTS

ACKNOWLEDGMENTS

Over the last several years, many people have given much blood, sweat and tears to bring the vision of Archangel to life. To my producers Jeff Burdett and Robin Chaudhuri, my sincerest thanks for being in my corner. And to the countless artists, actors, technicians, fellow filmmakers, and friends, who have brought their creativity to this project, thank you for making this dream come true.

-Dave Di Pietro, Reel Cool Entertainment

Archangel could never have come to life like it has without the support and understanding of my patient and lovely wife Michelle and my two beautiful daughters Savannah and Josie. We all hope you enjoy the adventure.

-Robin Chaudhuri, Reel Cool Entertainment

PROLOGUE

STILLNESS IS NOT ENTIRELY SILENT, FOR IT FORCES THE BRAIN to strain for sound: whispers, ringing, ghost-voices. When darkness is added to it, it manufactures shapes, as well. It presses against the face and clogs the senses. It tells you something is there when it is not and hides what things exist in the space you inhabit.

The escapee stood in such a dark stillness now, listening, trying to breathe silently, struggling to see what was really in the room with him and not what his imagination perversely insisted on putting there. If he gave in to his imagination, the big, dark room would fill up with monsters instead of dormant machinery.

He heard sounds—real ones, he thought—distantly. Voices raised in alarm. The clanging of an alarm bell. They must have discovered his escape.

He moved deeper into the cavernous lab, feeling his way carefully through the gauntlet of machine consoles and worktables. He knew there was a set of doors on the opposite wall of the room and prayed desperately that he would not become disoriented and miss them. His precious notes were in a drawer in the worktable just to the right of those doors and he could not—*would not*—leave here without them. If the Legion's so-called scientists remained in possession of those notes, there would be no end to the horrors they might unleash.

Abusing my work. Polluting it to create God-knows-what.

He nearly muttered the words aloud, caught himself, and moved forward again, keeping the doors he had used to enter the lab to his back. The tense gloom glided over his skin, and his ears imagined they heard a diffuse, high-pitched hissing sound as he sometimes experienced when startled from sleep. He patted his hip pocket, reassuring himself that his makeshift weapon was still there. Silly really. Where might it have gone? Since he'd used it to defeat the electro-magnetic lock on the door of his "guest room," he'd used it twice more—once to deal with the snoozing guard assigned to the hallway outside his room, once to penetrate this laboratory. He'd only just returned it to his pocket.

Someone shouted again. The sound was much closer now and accompanied by the thud of boots on stone. His pursuers were in the corridor he'd just left. Heart pounding, breath quickening, he moved more swiftly, trying not to shuffle his feet or trip over a stray chair. He kept his hands in front of him, fingers questing.

He came into sudden, jarring contact with a worktable, nearly crying out in his startlement. The shouts were even nearer, now. He stretched out his hand, praying his fingertips would meet the cold stone of the far wall. They did.

Galvanized, now, he felt along the front of the table for a drawer. He found one, pulled out his little tool and sent an arc of electrical energy into the lock. The lock surrendered and he yanked the drawer open. His blind fingers met a series of unknown objects, but no paper-filled folio. He slid sideways, opening the next drawer in the same manner. If they had moved the papers, put them in some secret hiding place . . . .

They hadn't. His questing hands met the soft leather of his folio and snatched it up. Pressing it to his breast, he pushed the drawers closed, sidled to the left end of the worktable, and used the tool again to defeat the lock on the next set of doors. Then he pushed through the doors into a corridor beyond.

This was *terra incognita*. He had only ever been from his room to the lab and back again. He paused for a split second to tally what he knew. He knew that somewhere to his right was a large courtyard where vehicles passed to and fro. If he was going to escape this madhouse, he must reach one of those vehicles.

There was nothing for it, then. He must go blindly into the unknown. "Here," he murmured, "there be dragons."

Turning toward the rear of the building, he pushed inexorably toward the unseen courtyard, counting his progress in years, constantly aware of the sounds of search now issuing from the lab. It sounded as if they were turning the place upside-down. They must suspect he was hiding there. Perhaps they would waste sufficient time trying to discover him in the huge room that he might increase the distance between them.

He'd been feeling his way along a wall when he encountered another set of doors. He pushed at them, finding them unlocked—indeed, unlatched. He hesitated only a moment before slipping through them. It was noticeably colder here and he could smell soot, cold stone, and metal. There was also a faint light seeping around the edges of yet another pair of doors. This was the source of the light in the broader corridor. He moved tentatively toward the beckoning exit, aware that there was now brick underfoot instead of polished stone, and that the air was much colder.

His heart beating so heavily he feared he might pass out, he pressed himself against the doors and listened. Sounds of human occupation, yes, but at a distance. The dominant sound was that of steam engines.

Quaking, he pushed one door open just enough to peek through. Before him was a warehouse whose far end opened into the courtyard. Steam lorries were backed up to what he assumed was a loading dock, presumably to pick up cargo. Between the lorries and where he stood was a collection of large crates in various stages of packing. The ones that had not yet been buttoned up seemed to be overflowing with straw and excelsior.

Knowing hesitation could quite literally kill him, he slipped through the doors and into the warehouse to lose himself among the crates.

ONE - RESISTANCE

LONDON

THE JOB WAS BORING. MARCH TO THE WESTERN CORNER OF THE building, exchange high signs with the man on the rooftop across the alley, turn and march back again, trade bored looks with Gus Tildon, wait expectantly for exactly two minutes (as if anything was likely to happen), then turn and repeat the entire process.

Sometimes Archie thought he should have kept working in his family's butcher shop. He'd joined this outfit because he thought it would be exciting work and because he'd always fancied a uniform. These uniforms, with their dark fabric and shiny buttons, were quite dashing, but the closest he'd come to exciting was laying eyes on the sort of cargo that got delivered to the rear of the store below and once catching sight of the Warlord himself—Cross, his name was.

Archie took a deep breath and remembered another minus of his job— the smell. Refuse, brine, and wet tar. A fine stew of scents, that was. His dad's butcher shop always smelt of wood soap and smoked meats.

Archie counted his steps to the western corner, wondering if it was too late to patch things up with his old man. He reached the corner and raised his thumb to signal the fellow on the roof.

There was no fellow on the roof. There was only empty, leaden grey sky.

He turned to shout something to Tildon about the rooftop bloke taking a leak, but Tildon was lying on the walkway in a pool of blood.

Archie froze. Only for a second, but it was a second too long. Before he could raise the alarm, he heard a whisper of sound behind him and felt a searing pain in his back, then another in his side. Without understanding how he had come to be lying flat on his back on the cold stone of the walkway, he found himself looking up into a face of which he could see only the eyes. The rest was shrouded in darkness.

A moment later, the face was gone, and Archie saw only the leaden sky and the rooftop across the alleyway, which was no longer empty. Standing atop it now was a figure from a nightmare—a dark, hooded phantom with huge glowing amber eyes, segmented scales that gleamed like brass, and black, billowing robes . . . or perhaps they were wings?

Was this the Angel of Death?

As a lethal sleep overtook him, Archie felt a moment of deep regret, knowing beyond doubt that it was too late to patch things up with his old man.

Colonel John Horan peered up the fogbound alley, squinting despite his goggles. From his vantage point in the sidecar of the motorcycle his man was piloting through the narrow London byway, he could already see the rear entrance of the shop that served to cover Legion activity. What he beheld annoyed him. Surrounded by a team of armed guards, a flatbed steam lorry sat behind the shop, its unloading overseen by a gang boss named Mullin. But what the damned man was overseeing at the moment was two of his lowlife workers lounging against one of the crates they were supposed to be ferrying into the shop. Horan struck his driver on the thigh and signaled for him to drive faster.

Mullin stood up in the driver's seat of the lorry as the motorcycle came to a stop and waved at Horan quite as if nothing was amiss. Horan climbed out of the sidecar, all but grinding his teeth.

"Mullin! What are these men doing just lolling about?"

Mullin blinked at him with bovine dullness. "Well, Colonel, it's just that hoisting these crates ain't light work. The men were complaining that they needed a breather."

One of the workers raised his bum from the side of the crate and shot Horan a gap-toothed grin. "That's right, Colonel. Me and Nate were just taking a quick fiver. This is hard work, isn't it? Man needs a rest."

"Does he?" said Horan, smiling now, himself. "Well, then, why don't you have a nice, *long* rest?"

Horan pulled his sidearm and shot the man square in the chest with a blast of energy, catapulting him backwards. He landed at the feet of a quartet of men who had congregated in the door of the shop on their way to unload more of the crates.

When the echoes of the gunshot had died, Horan turned a cold eye toward Mullin. The gang boss stared at him for no more than a second before turning to bark out orders to the remaining men.

"Oi! Come on then, you sorry lot! Pick up the pace!"

Silent as the newly dead, they hastened to do just that, not one of them looking at Horan or at the body they had to step around to reach the steam carriage.

Horan holstered his weapon, his eyes drifting to the signage over the back door of the shop. G.A. STRANGWAYS COFFIN MAKERS, it read. Horan threw back his head and laughed.

The man on the rooftop did not like to think of himself as the Angel of Death, though he granted that he had been forced to become that to great measure. He had been Lieutenant Colonel Brenden Winter once—a valued member of Her Majesty's Secret Intelligence Service, working to protect the Crown and the people of Great Britain from any and all enemies.

Brenden Winter was dead as far as the outside world was concerned, and had been replaced with *this*—this thing that moved in shadows and inspired fear . . . and hope, if he was to be honest. Brenden Winter had been exchanged for Archangel . . . or consumed by it. Now, he was only Brenden Winter on the inside. Just barely.

He watched the scene in the alley below, soberly marking the cheapness of life. Three guards and a hapless laborer had died already this night, and there might yet be more casualties. Archangel added three of those lives to his own account and wondered if he ought to feel more regret. The lenses of his night goggles had afforded him a look into the face of the last guard to die. He'd been barely more than a boy.

He shook off the moment and tapped a button on the side of his face mask, bringing its enhanced night-vision optics back online. He could see the alley behind the coffin maker's shop with stunning clarity now. He used a tiny dial near the outer edge of the right eye socket to zoom in on the scene, counting the well-armed Legion soldiers and the unarmed laborers, and taking special measure of the Legion colonel who had just slain a laborer for reasons Archangel found unfathomable.

"Sir Henry," he murmured, his voice barely audible to his own ears, "are the boys ready?"

"Yes, sir. Everyone is set." The reply came through the tiny diaphragms in the ear pieces of Archangel's helm; Sir Henry Ramsay was yards away on the ground, commanding his unit of the Resistance team.

"Right. On my move, then."

Archangel turned back to the alley, where the Legion colonel paced like an expectant father, checking and rechecking his pocket watch. As the unseen observer watched, the colonel turned to his driver and spoke.

"Sergeant."

"Sir!" The man came smartly to attention.

"I need you to contact headquarters and tell them—"

The colonel got no further in his command. Archangel moved on the word "contact," dropping from his perch down into the alley directly behind the driver. He saw the colonel's eyes go wide even as he used his momentum to deal the driver a savage blow to the back of his neck. He heard the snap of bone and knew the man was dead on his feet.

Snarling, the officer drew his weapon and opened fire. Archangel had expected that. He caught the driver's body as it sagged back toward him, using the unfortunate corpse as a shield against the lethal bolts of energy. His body armor was designed to withstand some weapons fire, but not from a pistol that could throw a full-grown man ten feet from the point of contact.

On cue, the alley around them erupted in chaos as Ramsay's men broke from hiding with guns blazing. Amid the thunder and sizzle of weaponry, the flash and fire of energy rounds, the Legionnaires dove for cover. The colonel rolled beneath the carriage of the lorry, while the man he'd called

Mullin roared aloud, produced a bulky rifle from under the driver's seat, then sought shelter behind it. He began to fire into the alley, trying to hit the Resistance fighters.

Archangel drew his sword from its metal scabbard and began to hack his way toward the rear of the coffin maker's shop. He'd taken no more than three strides when a half-dozen Legion soldiers swarmed through the doorway.

Well, perhaps swarmed was not quite the right word. The rather narrow aperture forced them to exit single file, making them prey to both the Resistance fighters' energy blasts and Archangel's sword. He cut his way through them, drawing closer and closer to the open doorway.

His forward progress was checked as a spray of energy bolts rained down from above, taking an indiscriminate toll on the men below. Archangel flung himself under the eaves of the shop and peered up into the dark sky. The oblate form of a Legion sentry balloon loomed over the battle, showering the alley with bolts of energy that, judging by how ill-aimed they were, likely came from the muzzles of auto-blasters. The Legion, Archangel knew, did not hesitate to sacrifice their own men in the cause of securing resources they felt were more precious.

Archangel touched a switch on the vambrace that covered his right forearm. It began to vibrate, sending tremors all the way to the marrow of his bones and making a sound that he'd come to imagine as the rage of mechanical bees. In seconds, the buzzing whine reached a crescendo. Archangel raised his arm toward the sentry balloon, sighting between his gloved knuckles, and clenched his fist—hard.

A blast of supercharged electrical energy shot upward toward the balloon's gondola. In the instant before it struck, it illuminated the face of the pilot, his eyes locked on the scene below. It exploded against the side of the gondola in a flash of intense light and heat. The gondola bucked and burst into flame. Traceries of fire raced up the rigging and onto the canopy, which disintegrated in a super-heated blossom of blinding intensity.

The shock wave felled several of the combatants, the heat was almost unbearable. In the seconds of confusion that followed, Archangel took several long strides and leapt aboard the steam lorry, bringing himself masked face to face with the gang boss, Mullin.

"What the hell are you?" the man snarled, his eyes reflecting the rain of fiery debris and honest fear.

In answer, Archangel ripped the rifle from Mullin's beefy hands and flung it aside. Despite his fear, the big man did not surrender. He reached down and grabbed a lethal-looking grapple, swinging it toward Archangel's hooded head. Powerful he might be, but he was not as quick as the shadow man he now faced. Archangel grasped the grapple as it arced toward him and moved with, not against, the momentum of the arc. In a heartbeat, Mullin was airborne, flying headfirst toward a collision with the crate that sat, forgotten, between the lorry and the shop.

The impact shattered the top of the crate, splintering it into long, lethal slivers, sharp as a butcher's knives. Mullin, unwilling to surrender to Archangel, had instead surrendered to an inanimate killer.

Archangel had little time to react to his victory; the Legion colonel darted out of the shadow of the steam lorry, making a mad dash for his motorcycle. Archangel followed, jumping down from the lorry and landing lightly on the cobbles. He heard the roar of the motorcycle as he landed, and straightened to see the Legion officer gunning the cycle in a desperate attempt at escape. His flight was slowed by numerous obstacles: men locked in combat, flaming debris, weapons fire . . . his own sidecar. The rear of the cycle fishtailed on the damp cobbles as he tried to wend his way free of the battleground.

Sir Ramsay's men were still engaged with the last of the Legion soldiers. If the colonel was going to be kept from escaping and communicating with his HQ, the responsibility of stopping him had fallen to Archangel.

Archangel pelted down the alley after the cycle until he was clear of the fighting. Then he stepped to the center of the alley and pulled a tool from his belt. The device was circular and had a padded brace of the strongest steel that ran across the diameter of the circle. From it jutted a spring-activated grapple. Holding the device by the brace, Archangel aimed at the cyclist, again sighting through the knuckles of his vambrace glove.

When it seemed the officer had steadied the vehicle and was picking up speed, Archangel fired the grapple. The sharp, compact hook flew through the air, a high tensile filament of cable running out behind it from the launcher's circular spool. The arrow-sharp point of the grapple struck the colonel squarely in the back between the shoulder blades, thrusting clean through his body and exiting his chest.

He was dead before the grapple sprung open and on his way to Hell before he reached the end of the tether and his body was ripped from the cycle. The unmanned machine went on without him. Driverless, it flipped, tumbling down the alley until it impacted with the wall of one of the hemming buildings. It exploded, the ambient wash of light lapping over the colonel's still body.

Archangel detached the cable from the grapple launcher and hooked it back to his belt. Then he slipped into the shadows and made his way back up the alley to the coffin maker's shop.

The fighting had ended. Unsurprising. His men were trained to fight under chaotic circumstances. Still, he saw several bodies that wore the dark cloth and concealing scarves of the Resistance lying amid the debris. Living members of the unit were already gathering around the fallen, preparing to remove them from the alley so they would not be found by the local authorities.

As Archangel drew near the narrow battlefield, a tall, masked Resistance fighter approached him, lowering the scarf that hid his face. Its features were angular, even craggy, and full of hard-earned character.

"Sir Henry," Archangel greeted him.

"Not exactly the quietest or most elegant of operations, old boy." Sir Henry Ramsay gave the alley a sideways glance. The dark forms of corpses littered the way and fires here and there reflected in the glistening cobbles.

Archangel gave the area another look. "No, I should say not. We managed to make quite a mess." His eyes fell on Mullins' lifeless body where it lay atop the broken crate. Something protruded from beneath the big man that had the dark sheen of metal. "Hello. Come have a look at this."

He crossed to the crate, Ramsay following, and rolled the body onto the ground. Then he pulled away broken slats and packing material until he uncovered most of the metallic object he'd spotted. It was a weapon. A particularly lethal weapon, by the look of it, and one of many in the crate. A bolt rifle. He'd seen these blow a moving steam car right off the road.

He cleared away more of the packing material, revealing the crate's contents, then activated his optics' remote transmitter. "Artemus," he said, "are you seeing this?"

Two - Mage

LONDON - ST. PANCRAS

ARTEMUS McDOWELL LEANED CLOSER TO A SMALL, CIRCULAR tele-monitor at the center of an array of similar mechanisms set into his workstation. What he saw there, illumined by the night-vision optics in Archangel's face mask, made him whistle reflexively.

"Eloquent as always," said the man on the other end of the tele feed. "But is this the shipment you've been tracking?"

Artemus was aware that a couple of the lab's denizens had paused behind him to peer over his shoulder. He ignored them, cleared his throat, and spoke into the tele-monitor's audio-phone.

"Oh, yes. This is definitely the shipment that came in from Enfield. Bolt rifles, volta blades, vibronic disrupters, and a variety of mech-axes. A right diverse and jolly array of destruction."

The view in the tele swung to a dark, narrow doorway, then to a wet, debris-field amid which Resistance fighters went about the grim business of accounting for their dead and wounded.

"How long do we have before reinforcements arrive?" Archangel asked.

Artemus swept his gaze across several of the other monitors, each showing the view from a stationary mechanical "eye" trained on local intersections. He saw movement in two of them.

"I'd say no more than ten, maybe fifteen minutes. You'd best hurry."

"Right."

The point of view changed again and Artemus found himself looking into Henry Ramsay's solemn face.

Archangel spoke to his field marshal. "Sir Henry, have the men get these few remaining crates back on the wagon, as fast as we can. We need to get them undercover."

"On it."

Ramsay dodged out of the frame and Artemus was looking at the crate full of weaponry again.

"Will you be traveling with the shipment?" he asked, preparing himself to argue the point with his commander if he must.

He never received an answer. Instead of replying to the question, Archangel turned his head sharply toward a steam lorry that dominated the alley, said, "What was that?" then terminated the tele feed.

The little screen went blank. "Sir!" Artemus protested. He looked up at the blank monitor to see a red light blinking next to the speaking diaphragm.

Behind him, one of the persons looming over his shoulder chuckled. "You been muted, old man. Ain't that just like his nibs?"

"Yes, Kenzie, it is. I suppose I shall just have to get unmuted."

Artemus pulled what appeared to be a typewriter keyboard to the middle of his workbench. It was connected to the tele-monitors and support machinery by a braid of thin cable. He cracked his knuckles and began to manipulate the outgoing signal from his remote communications system.

Archangel tilted his head, listening intently to the aural input enhanced by the diaphragms in his helm. He interpreted that input as a series of coughs coming from the far side of the lorry. Specifically, he realized as he poked his head around the front end of the vehicle, it was coming from a crate that sat next to the lorry, apparently abandoned when fighting broke out.

As he prowled toward it, the box coughed yet again. A crowbar lay on the cobbles near the crate. Archangel picked it up and attacked the lid, prying it up to expose a layer of packing material. Before he could move to sweep any of the stuff aside, a man rose up out of the crate, coughing and sending excelsior and straw cascading onto the cobbles. The stowaway gaped at Archangel, let out a yip of alarm, and pointed a fountain pen at him. A split second later, a fitful burst of electricity arced from the pen to Archangel's chest plate. The stream was so weak, his body armor easily absorbed it.

"Oh, dear," said the man in the box. "Oh, damn. It's lost its charge."

Archangel stepped forward, grasped the fellow by the lapels of his coat and lifted him out of the crate in a veritable fountain of packing material. Setting the man on his feet, he demanded, "Who are you?"

His earpieces crackled to life just then and he heard a gasp, followed by Artemus's voice in his ear: "My word! Wait, Brenden! Wait! For God's sake, don't kill him!"

Archangel stifled his mild annoyance at the revelation that he was not solely in control of his technology, and asked, "Why ever not? He tried to kill me."

Artemus and the strange young man spoke in urgent harmony: "Nikola Tesla!"

"I'm Nikola Tesla," the man repeated. "And I'd only have stunned you."

Artemus cleared his throat and echoed, "He's Nikola Tesla."

"The scientist?" asked Archangel, studying the excelsior-covered apparition.

Tesla was studying him in return, peering intently at his face mask with its oversized amber lenses and the gleaming metal grillwork that covered the lower half of his face.

"Oh, wait," the scientist said. "You must be the one they call Archangel. May I hope that I'm being rescued?"

"That depends. What are you doing hiding inside a crate and in the possession of the Legion?"

"Trying very hard *not* to be in the possession of the Legion. I escaped from their laboratory. They were forcing me to work on a new type of electrical battery for a secret project—a weapon, I gather. I built this little energy weapon from some bits and bobs I pilfered from the lab and the loo, escaped my quarters, then hid in this outgoing shipment." His mouth twisted wryly. "It's ironic, really. If the room had had a mundane mechanical lock instead of an electromagnetic one, I'd still be a prisoner."

"I see," said Archangel. "What were you planning to do when your crate was opened?"

Tesla blinked several times as if the thought had only just occurred to him. The fear in his eyes was unmistakable.

"To be honest, I'm not sure. Obviously, I was prepared to stun someone . . . well, unless, of course, they were wearing some sort of body armor. Most interesting," he added, touching a finger to Archangel's segmented chest plate. "Beyond that, I suppose I would have thought of something. But at least I am out of that horrible place and away from those equally horrible people."

"Sir!"

Archangel turned to see Sir Henry and a half-dozen of his men approaching from the rear of the lorry. Seeing Tesla, they held their weapons at the ready. Seeing them, Tesla let out a gasp.

Archangel held up a gloved hand to signal his men to lower their weapons. "Don't be alarmed," he told the scientist. "These men are with me."

"All crates are loaded and ready to go, except this one," reported Ramsay, then peered at Tesla above his concealing scarf. "Who is this?"

Archangel turned back to Tesla. "May I introduce Sir Henry Ramsay. Sir Henry, Professor Nikola Tesla. We are apparently affecting his rescue."

Sir Henry rarely showed surprise. He did now. "Professor Tesla," he said, inclining his head in a show of respect. "A genuine honor, sir."

"No time for pleasantries," said Artemus in Archangel's ear. "You will soon have unpleasant company."

Archangel gestured at the scientist. "We need to get Professor Tesla to the safe house as soon as possible. And make sure this shipment gets to its final destination, minus a few of the 'extras.'"

"We're on it, sir." Ramsay turned to Tesla. "Dr. Tesla, we must hurry. Come with me."

Brushing straw out of his dark hair, the professor turned to offer Archangel a slight bow. "I thank you, sir. So very much. I can't tell you—" A look of fresh alarm passed over his face. "Oh, wait. My papers!"

He half-dove back into the crate, rummaging through the packing material until he came up with a thick leather-bound folio. Clutching the folio to his chest, Tesla gave Archangel a nod, which Archangel returned, his amusement hidden beneath his expressionless mask. He watched Ramsay escort the scientist away, then moved aside as the steam lorry hissed to life.

"Well, well," said Artemus into his earpiece. "It appears we have gotten more than we bargained for with this haul."

"Indeed. I am willing to wager that whatever papers Dr. Tesla deems so precious are also important to the Legion. Fate has dealt us a very strong hand tonight, Artemus. However, with every winner, there must also be a loser. And that loser will no doubt be out for blood."

THREE - CROSS

PARIS

MADAM JACQUELINE (WHO HAD NEVER GONE BY ANY MORE OF A name than that) looked out over the darkly colorful main room of her cabaret and took stock of her clientele. They enjoyed themselves anonymously for the most part, veiled in smoke from cigar, cigarette, and water pipe, features blurred and altered by the aura of rose-colored light that sprayed from well-placed gas lamps, their conversations swaddled in ambient noise from the stage and from their own mouths.

Tucked away in a dimly lit Paris side street, Maison Rosé was, if nothing else, a place to be seen while being neither seen or heard. Deals were made here, and Jacqueline made a point of knowing what those deals were. She had ways of knowing. She had reasons for knowing.

The stage show this night consisted of three mediocre dancing girls doing the can-can. Or at least something distantly approaching a can-can. Jacqueline doubted any of her patrons—eccentrics, everyone—even knew the girls existed. Their attention was focused on their particular business or pleasure.

Jacqueline, sipping at a mild sherry from a brandy snifter, looked up as an unfamiliar young man entered the club. She might not have marked him at all, he was so nondescript, except that he seemed anxious or fearful, his gaze darting here and there in the lurid, smoky room. He stopped a passing waiter, asking an obviously urgent question that the waiter answered by pointing to the far corner of the cabaret where a dim alcove was shielded from the rest of the room by the curving bar. The young man hurried in that direction, dodging other patrons.

Jacqueline suspected she knew whom the fellow sought. It was of interest to her, so she slipped behind the bar and moved to its far end at a leisurely and unexceptional pace, swirling the sherry in her snifter. At the far end of the bar, she stopped, took out a makeup mirror, and patted at her pale curls, all the while pretending to chat up a customer so far in his cups that he had fallen asleep with his chin wedged into his beer mug.

From this vantage point, Jacqueline saw the young stranger approach a tall, powerful-looking woman who was also, she had to admit, quite beautiful . . . if you liked beautiful things that were made of ice and possibly lethal. The woman's name was Daphne Bellanger. Jacqueline could not imagine anyone who looked less like a Daphne. Daphne was a fragrant, delicate flower that bloomed in the spring. The wintry Mademoiselle Bellanger was about as far from delicate as could be imagined.

Jacqueline turned her back to the alcove and tilted her little mirror so she could watch the encounter between the nervous man and Daphne the Ice Queen. She would never be able to hear their conversation over the rumble of the crowded room, but she could read their lips. She'd taught herself this useful ability just so she could know the sorts of things her customers were discussing.

Reaching the Bellanger woman, the nervous man drew a folded slip of paper from his pocket and handed it to her. "This just came in for Mr. Cross," he said. "It's urgent."

Daphne the Not Delicate, snatched the message from the man's hand, read it, and refolded it. Her facial expression somehow conveyed icy fury without having changed a whit.

"I'll take it to him. Tell them the pick-up will proceed on schedule at the new location. Get going."

The messenger nodded and left.

Jacqueline pocketed her mirror and retraced her steps to the end of the bar closest to the front door. There she waved to a pair of identical youths who sat at a small, round table sharing a hookah pipe. They looked up in eerie unison, and she made a quick gesture at the messenger who was just now slipping out through the front door.

The youths rose as if directed by a single mind and followed him from the club.

Daphne Bellanger turned on her heel and returned to the alcove beyond the bar, the damned message clutched in her hand. From the corner of her eye, she caught the proprietress tucking away her pocket mirror. Daphne's lip curled. There was no amount of makeup made that would render that vain old tart palatable.

Daphne paused in the mouth of the shallow recess, taking in the tableau at its center. On an ornate couch flanked by two Legion guards, Benton Cross sat between a pair of his exotic "birds," soaking up their doe-eyed regard, their flattery, their sultry laughter, and their purchased kisses. The low table before them was laden with drinks and *hors d'oeuvres*. The two women hung on Cross as if they were clothing draped haphazardly on a cloak stand.

Angry for reasons she told herself had nothing to do with the whores and everything to do with the message she held, Daphne strode forward, grabbed one of the women by her soft, fleshy arm, and tore her away from Cross. The woman landed on her buttocks on the floor in a pile of silken petticoats, swearing violently in French—or rather swearing as violently as one could in a language so soft and rounded. Good swearing, Daphne thought, required consonants with jagged edges and hard, blunt surfaces. English and German—now, those were languages fit for swearing.

Cross pouted, sending Daphne a smoky look from his dark eyes. "Now, now. Don't play so rough, my love. These are pricey toys."

Daphne leaned down and put her lips against his ear. He smiled as if expecting a kiss. Instead she said, "Tesla has escaped and the shipment has been compromised." Then she straightened and watched his face, gratified by the way the soporific haze of desire and the arrogant smile were swept away as if by a silent wind.

"What!?"

He rose violently, overthrowing the table in front of him and sending its contents crashing to the floor. His rage unspent, he turned to the second girl, who had risen with him, and tumbled her to the floor amid the mess. She cried out in pain as she fell onto broken glass, then commenced to wail.

This got the attention of her mistress, who had come from behind the bar to steam toward the alcove like a ship-of-the-line, skirts billowing like sails. Cross started to aim a kick at the fallen whore, but Daphne dug her fingernails into his shoulder, distracting him. He snarled and shot her a look that could melt stone. Fortunately, she was made of something harder than that.

"It's all right," she told him, one eye on the madam's approach. "Our agent has informed us where the shipment is being held."

Cross ground his teeth. "Tesla?"

"The little bookworm managed to get clean away. I'm certain he's in the hands of the Resistance."

"How?"

Madame Jacqueline had reached them by now and was huddled with her two girls, cooing over them like a mother dove with a pair of gaudy chicks. Daphne took a firm grip on Cross's upper arm and steered him to the farthest corner of the alcove behind one of the guards.

"Our shipment was ambushed at the distribution site, the weapons were taken and the unit leader was killed. Tesla had apparently hidden himself in one of the crates in the outgoing shipment."

"How can this happen?" Cross demanded. "I made Lord Atherton Regent, but the man is an incompetent fool who cannot, apparently, oversee the simplest of operations." He paused, thinking, his fine mouth drawn into a resolute line. "Contact the Red Tong."

"What?" Daphne let go of his arm. "Why would we need those bloody skyraiders?"

"Because I'm tired of losing *my* men. Let Judd and his rabble retrieve the shipment. If we lose some of them, so be it. Tell him to meet us at Rotherwood."

Daphne could not fault his logic. "What about Atherton?"

The smile Cross gave her was at once grim and vile. "I think it's time I paid a visit to my worthless little lackey. Ready my ship; I want to leave for England within the hour. Though not without company, I think," he added, turning his gaze to the madam and her sniveling whores.

Madame Jacqueline had succeeded in getting the injured girl to her feet with the help of her colleague. She raised her chin arrogantly and looked Cross in the eye.

"I should charge you double," she told him. "You've not only ruined their dresses, but Claire must see the surgeon."

Cross made a dismissive gesture. "Whatever you want, Jackie, old girl. You're right. These two are quite ruined. Get me two fresh ones and have them brought to my ship."

Jacqueline's painted mouth tightened, but she gave Cross a subservient nod. "Certainly, *monsieur.*"

Cross turned back to Daphne then. "Well, what are you waiting for, Daf? Go!"

She went.

Having delivered his message to the Bellanger woman (who never failed to terrify him), Etienne Barnier hurried along the moonlit Parisian streets, zigging and zagging this way and that as he'd been taught, yet working himself inexorably toward his destination. He made a turn into an alley so narrow, he doubted two men could walk abreast if they were much larger than he.

He had the sudden impression that he was being observed and looked up from the stone of the alley floor. A slender youth dressed in a green velvet coat stood before him in the center of the way. He was no more than twenty, Etienne thought, and looked ridiculously out of place in the gritty dark of the alley. He was certainly no footpad.

Etienne decided against traveling this alley, after all. He did an about-face and started back in the opposite direction, then stopped and gaped. Standing on the sidewalk at the end of the alley illumined by a street lamp was the same youth, wearing the same velvet coat, but in a shade of vibrant blue.

Surely not, though. Surely it was pure imagination that made the two look so alike, or rendered their coats in different hues.

Etienne turned sideways to put his back to the wall of a building, and looked to his right. The other youth was still there, and now emerged from the darkness into the dim light of the street lamp. Now Etienne could see that his coat really was green. He turned his head toward the street; Blue Boy was also in motion, approaching silently.

It was that silence that unnerved Etienne. What could they possibly want with him?

"If it's money you're after," he told them, "I have none."

"No," said Blue Boy, "we are not—"

"After your money," his doppelgänger finished.

Etienne's unease grew. He pressed himself against the wall as the two hemmed him in, and when each reached out a hand to touch his face in perfect synchronicity, his confusion was complete. They did not lay violent hold of him, but instead merely rested their fingertips upon the sides of his face and closed their eyes.

What came next was like nothing Etienne had ever experienced. He felt as if the fingers so lightly pressed against his temples had worked their way through his skull into the meat of his brain. Then came a sensation as if an ooze of warm water was running through his head. He whimpered as that ooze became a trickle, and that trickle became a current, and that current became a maelstrom.

He tried to scream, hoping a gendarme might hear him, but the scream came out of his mouth a warped and muted mew.

"Calm yourself," said Blue Boy, and Etienne realized he knew the youth's name. It was Aidan.

How could he know that?

"Just tell us what you know—" Green Boy said.

"—about what the Legion is planning," Aidan finished. "This does not need—"

"—to be too painful."

The last thing that Etienne Barnier knew was that Green Boy's name was Ethan.

FOUR - WINTER

LONDON - CLARE MARKET

THE STREETS OF LONDON WERE TEEMING WITH PEOPLE. THEY always were in the morning hours when cooks and scullery maids and housewives went about their daily shopping. Gazing down St. Clement's Street toward the Strand, Brenden Winter felt a profound sense of astonishment that Clare Market looked the same as it ever had before the Legion had tightened its shadowy grip on government.

You had to look for the real difference, had to notice how many Legion soldiers there were mixed into the crowd and how many constables there were not. Queen Victoria, God rest her soul, should never have allowed Parliament to dissolve the Bow Street Runners. After her assassination, the infant constabulary of Scotland Yard had been no match for Benton Cross's well-funded forces.

Seeing a pair of soldiers wending their way up the sidewalk toward where he stood, Winter took the precaution of turning away to consider the wares of a peanut roaster who'd set his cart up before a bakery on the row. Winter was in disguise, dressed head-to-foot in the sort of shabby, but tasteful clothing an English physician might wear. In fact, as far as the people passing him by knew, he was Dr. Heywood Atkinson of St. Pancras. They would not know that the valise he carried contained only the bare minimum of medical implements. Beneath the bag's false bottom were items that would very definitely do harm.

He watched the soldiers in the window of the bakery as they passed by, giving his own altered visage a glance to be sure nothing would give him away. His hair was drabbed almost to gray with a special powder, while on his face, he wore a thin film of the mastic developed by a Scottish chemist named MacIntosh that did a fine job of appearing to wrinkle the skin. A pair of spectacles and a top hat completed the costume.

"Will ye have something then, sir?" the peanut vendor asked.

"Ah, yes." Winter nodded. "I believe I will have a bag."

As the vendor filled a paper bag with roasted nuts, Winter got out his purse and dug out a bit more than the amount advertised on the piece of cardboard the vendor had propped up on the handle of his cart. As he counted out the change, he glanced up the street, marking the soldiers' passing. He could no longer see them, but he could see the eddy they caused in the crowd as people turned aside or drew back from their path or altered course to avoid them. A little girl sat on the curb near the peanut vendor's cart, drawing on the sidewalk with a piece of chalk. If she'd noticed the soldier's passage, she showed no sign of it.

It was interesting—or perhaps horrific was a better word—how constant terror changed a society. For none were more hopelessly enslaved than those who falsely believed they were free. He doubted the good Londoners even noticed how they tacitly accepted the presence of the Legion in their midst, as if refusing to look directly at them rendered them invisible and impotent.

Winter paid the vendor and took his bag of hot peanuts, noticing a poster on the bakery wall to the left of the cart. It was torn and filthy, though the event it commemorated was as grand as England could muster: the funeral of her beloved Queen. It was her face, round yet regal, that dominated the poster. Some had likened her to a bulldog. She had certainly been as stubborn as one and as brave—determined to fight the Legion and refusing to be coopted or intimidated by it.

It was this refusal to be bought or terrorized that had ultimately led to her death . . . and his.

Head inclined toward the window; I watched the swiftly passing scenery outside the train car that carried me toward London. An observer might assume I was mesmerized by it. I was not, though I was using the rhythmic cadence of wheels on track to center my thoughts. I was awaiting a signal. A signal that would mark the beginning of the end of a most secret mission.

The 'Special' part of my agency was the nature of my covert duties. In plain, unvarnished terms, I was an assassin for the Crown, sworn to protect that Crown and the head it sat upon at any cost. It was because of this that I found my most recent assignment disturbing. The train in which I rode was the Royal train. The car in which I sat was but one removed from the car that carried the Queen and her party.

What this suggested to me was that the enemy I had been assigned to neutralize was very close to the Queen and might even be an intimate member of her inner circle. I thought that unlikely. At least, I hoped it was not so. Such betrayal could not help but have a profound effect on our Queen. More likely it was a servant or functionary whose role placed them close to Her Majesty, but who had been corrupted by the Legion.

I use the word 'neutralize' to describe my task. This is a safe word, an unpretentious word, meant to disguise the reality. I was used to disguises and wore them frequently, as I did today. Today, my disguise made me a bearded and mustachioed diplomat; my reality made me an assassin.

A chime sounded from the pocket of my coat. I whisked out my pocket watch and checked the time. Yes. I must move now, and with precision. My handler had told me that the target would be alone in the receiving parlor of the Queen's private car in five minutes time.

In a well-practiced movement, I grasped the crown of the codex ring I wore on my left hand and turned the signet to form a key of sorts. This I pressed into a round depression in the panel below the window. The panel dropped, revealing a small, but deadly weapon—an energy-enhanced projectile pistol—which I quickly retrieved and slipped into the pocket of my coat. Then I rose and left my compartment to make my way up the train's narrow passage toward the Queen's car.

I stepped out onto the jointed access platform between the two cars. Here, the noise of wheels on track was deafening. I ignored the sudden barrage of sound and peered through the glass into the small vestibule where the Queen's guards were stationed. There was only one guard and I did not recognize him. I damn well should recognize him. I was supposed to know every person in proximity to Queen Victoria. Hair stood up on the back of my neck, putting every sense I possessed on high alert.

Had the enemy moved before the SIS had been able to mount a preemptive strike? Was the Queen, even now, in danger?

I took a centering breath and opened the door to the guard's cabin. The man, stone-faced, held up a hand to halt me from going farther. I flipped up the lapel of my coat and gestured at the insignia pinned to the underside.

"SIS," I said. "I need to check on the Queen."

"No you don't," the man countered. His hand twitched toward his sidearm.

I moved with a speed honed by years of training and practice and dealt him a sharp blow to the stomach. When he doubled over, I grasped his head in both hands and simply snapped his neck. It was a thing I had learned to do without thought.

The body dropped; I left it where it lay. It was doubtful, but there might be evidence somewhere on it that could lead to the man's superiors.

I drew my gun now and moved on into the car. A narrow L-shaped hallway connected the guard's cabin to the royal receiving parlor. I leaned back against the wall just outside the chamber and checked my watch. The target should now be alone within.

I stepped into the parlor, raised my weapon, and froze. Staring back at me from an elegant settee, was a gray-haired woman with a round face that spoke volumes about tenacity and resolve. In the moment that she opened her mouth to speak to me—a moment in which I wondered if I should drop my gun and fall at her feet—I heard the muffled discharge of a weapon. The Queen of England fell sideways onto her couch, blood blossoming from a wound in the center of her chest.

A projectile weapon had made that wound, and I was certain the weapon was identical to the one I held in my hand. I had been set up. She had been set up.

Sensing a presence behind me, I crouched and spun about, reaching up to grasp the assassin's gun hand by the wrist. The damned thing must have been aimed at my head. I had no leverage in this position, but I was able to hook my left leg behind the assassin's, toppling him to the floor. The gun discharged a second time and I felt a searing pain as the round grazed my ribs.

Calling up all my reserves, I kicked the gun from the man's hand, aimed my own weapon at my adversary's torso and fired. He crumpled like a sodden rag, leaving me alone in the car with the Queen's body.

Sounds from the opposite end of the car told me I would not be alone for long. I glanced at the blood of my own wound seeping through the fabric of my coat, felt it run wetly down my side. I was too badly injured to fight, and these were not the people I should

be fighting, in any case. I had no option but to flee and nowhere to flee but the country-
side we sped through.

"To the Queen!" someone shouted.

I turned and retraced my steps to the guard cabin and from there to the access
platform. I was losing both blood and consciousness; my extremities felt as if ice
had penetrated my bones. I hesitated but a moment to send up a prayer for my wife and
son, then flung myself from the moving train to the wooded hillside below.

If the Legion wanted me dead, perhaps I would oblige them.

Someone stumbled against Winter, jarring him out of his grim reverie
and almost causing him to drop the bag of peanuts that were still pleas-
antly warming his hands.

"Sorry, mate! You all right?" The gravelly voice belonged to a man in a
hooded greatcoat, who was even now steadying Winter with both hands.

Winter looked up into a familiar face. "Yes, yes. Sorry if I was in the
way. Just a bit lost in thought, I suppose."

"Or perhaps just lost," said Sir Henry wryly. "I hope you find what
you're looking for." He patted Winter's breast pocket and smiled.

"Why, yes," Winter said. "I'm sure I will."

"Good day to you, sir," Sir Henry said and added, in more subdued
tones, "God Bless the Queen!"

Winter watched him walk away into the Clare Market, then turned
to resume his own journey. He'd gone no more than three strides before the
entire atmosphere of the market changed. Quite suddenly there were three
times as many Legion soldiers on the street as there had been moments
before. They began to block off passageways, side streets and alleys, and
cordoned off St. Clements above and below the market. He'd no doubt
they were doing the same on Clare.

The question was why?

FIVE - LEGION

LONDON - CLARE MARKET

THE PEOPLE INSIDE THE LEGION CORDON REACTED TO THE soldiers' presence in diverse ways. Some disappeared into storefronts, reasoning, Winter thought, that even as many Legionnaires as now inhabited the market couldn't see everyone. Others cried out, or went stock still in fear, or murmured to their companions. Some simply continued to conduct their business as the Legionnaires did not exist.

The little girl who'd been drawing chalk pictures looked up at the soldiers with a face that might as well have been made of stone. She added a new pictogram to her collection: a crude version of the Resistance insignia for Archangel. Winter found the sight almost cheering, for it meant the child—and likely her parents—wasn't numb to their condition, but only unwilling to reveal her true feelings about it. She'd make a good spy when she was grown, he thought, then realized what that implied—that too many years would pass before the Legion lost its growing stranglehold on British society.

An officer—a colonel Winter recognized as Archibald Gerrish—saw the girl and planted his booted foot atop the image she'd drawn, grinding it into the pavement. The girl did not quail. She gazed up into the colonel's face, her own expression reminding Winter of another, equally resolute stare.

"Whose child is this?" the officer demanded.

A woman bulled her way through the crowd to scoop up the little girl, giving her a swat for getting in the "good officer's" way. She apologized profusely, bowed her head, and carried the silent child away and into the bakery. The shrill sound of the shop bell was cut off by the closing of the door.

The colonel looked after her, a sneer on his narrow face. Then he appropriated a shoe-shine boy's crate, stepped up onto it, and addressed the Legionnaires at his command.

"Men! No one leaves this area until I say so! If anyone tries, shoot them!" He paused to let that sink in, ignoring the gasps and grumbling that rippled through the crowd, then went on. "Most of you know me, but for those few who may not, I am Colonel Gerrish of the Legion's Elite City Force!"

There was more grumbling, some of it woven with colorful suggestions of what Colonel Gerrish might do to himself. He ignored the grumbles—if indeed he heard them at all—and explained the reason for the Legion's sudden interest in the Clare Market.

"It has been brought to our attention that there is a high-ranking Resistance leader in the marketplace today. And that he may be carrying information regarding the whereabouts of a foreign dissident scientist by the name of Tesla."

The people around Winter began to look at each other, as if wondering which of their neighbors might be a Resistance spy. Winter joined in the pantomime, his gaze sweeping the area until it fell on Ramsay, who was standing in the doorway of a poulterer's shop on the opposite side of the street. Winter hesitated for only a moment, before continuing his survey, ostensibly peering suspiciously at strangers, but in reality assessing the forces Gerrish had brought with him. There were at least twenty City Force soldiers visible from where Winter stood. He was certain there were more he couldn't see.

He completed the visual sweep and turned back to the colonel to find the man's cold eyes locked on him. Without breaking eye contact, Gerrish stepped down from the shoe shine box and made his way to where Winter was standing. Face to face, the Legion officer looked him up and down.

"I know you, don't I? . . . . Yes. Dr. Atkinson, isn't it?"

Winter nodded deferentially and smiled. "Why yes, Colonel. I must say you have an excellent memory."

"Your office-residence is in St. Pancras, is it not? What brings you to this part of town?"

"I am on my way to pick up some laudanum at the chemist on Fleet Street. My local supplier was fresh out."

Gerrish pursed his lips thoughtfully. "I see. But there are at least three other chemists between St. Pancras and here. Do I assume that they are also fresh out?"

Winter chuckled. "Oh, no, nothing of the sort. You see, Harry Thorndike owns the shop on Fleet Street. He's an old friend of mine. Besides, it's less than a two-mile walk. I thought I might combine my medical mission with my constitutional and a friendly visit in time for tea."

"Ah. And do you always bring your medical satchel with you when you visit the chemist for tea?"

"Oh!" Winter looked down at said satchel and affected a befuddled look as if he was surprised to find it in his hand. "My goodness. Force of habit, I suppose. But a fortuitous habit; I can use it to carry away the laudanum."

"Indeed? Then I am sure you will not mind if I inspect the contents of your bag?"

Winter shrugged. "Not at all. It contains only my traveling medical equipment."

"Then this will take but a moment."

Gerrish slowly reached for the bag. Winter's hand tightened reflexively around the handle. While the false bottom was quite clever, a man like Gerrish, who was already suspicious, might discern it. If he did, Winter was trapped. Neither shackles nor prison could bind him as effectively as the throng of innocents surrounding him.

The colonel's fingertips had barely grazed the bag when there was a great hue and cry on the opposite side of the street. Several Legion soldiers were barging through the crowd, one of them roaring for someone to stop. Pulling the medical satchel back, Winter raised his head to see Sir Henry Ramsay dodging market-goers and soldiers alike, making for the narrow opening of an alley down toward the Strand.

Gerrish was no longer interested in Dr. Atkinson's satchel. He turned toward the brouhaha and shouted after his men: "Stop that man! *Stop him!*"

Ramsay was not to be caught easily, however. As Winter watched, he led the soldiers a wild chase, leaping, pivoting, landing blows when necessary. He had almost made the alley when he attempted to use a clothier's kiosk to launch himself to a first floor balcony. The kiosk collapsed beneath him, sending him to the cobbles in a tangle of fabric. The Legion soldiers descended on him like vultures.

Winter dove back into the crowd, wending his way toward where Ramsay struggled against the City Guard. From behind a cutler's stall, he saw the older man attempt to extract something small from his pocket. Winter's very soul writhed at the sight. He knew what Sir Henry, the best of friends and fighters, meant to do.

So, apparently, did Gerrish. Arriving at the spot, he snatched the capsule from Ramsay's fingers, then dealt his head a stunning blow with the butt of his pistol.

Winter swallowed bile as the colonel pulled the hood away from the unconscious man's face and turned to his men with a smug expression.

"Sir Henry Ramsay. Of course. I should have expected him." He looked down at the poison pill he held in his gloved hand. "No, sir. You will not get away from me that easily. Take him to Rotherwood."

He made a dismissive gesture with the hand that held the capsule, then tucked it into his pocket before turning to survey the crowd. Though Winter had moved, Gerrish found him and met his gaze across the many yards that now separated them. After a moment of grim study, Gerrish affected a crooked smile, touched the brim of his cap, and turned away, collecting his "elite forces" as he went.

Six - Regent

REGENT'S PALACE - ROTHERWOOD

THE REGENT'S ESTATE AT ROTHERWOOD WAS THE VERY DEFINITION of palatial. The home itself—a Georgian manor with older Norman and Tudor sections that had been skillfully updated and blended in—was a massive affair seated in acres of manicured gardens and stately woodlands like a gem in a bed of green velvet. The velvet was a bit faded now, owing to the cold, but it detracted little from the majesty of the place. At this time of day, with frost cloaking the greenery and stonework, it sparkled as if built of crystal. The only things that detracted from the picture of bucolic grandeur, Daphne thought, were the two large skyships hovering overhead.

For just a moment, as she and her party were escorted beneath the portico and into the receiving hall, she let herself pretend that this was her palace and that she was the lady of it. That the guards and servants and gleaming stone and woodwork, the capacious rooms and the rich fabrics belonged to her. She wondered if she looked as if she belonged to them. If she did, it meant she was a good liar. In her youth, she could never have imagined she would ever even enter such a place. She had been expected by those who knew her as a sullen child prone to daydreaming, to follow in her mother's footsteps—to be a second-rate actress and "dancer."

The only dancing her mother had done had been between the sheets. Daphne Bellanger had decided early in life that she would not be a second-rate anything or to accept her mother's fate as her own. So, she had studied fencing with the great Master Jean-Louis Michel in Montpellier, had entered tournaments and won them. At first she had disguised herself as a boy, but as she won one tournament after another, she was able to throw aside her disguise and accept the acknowledgment that she wielded the deadliest sword in all of Europe.

Still, she took nothing for granted. Her position was not something she felt was her due because of who she was, but something she had earned because of what she had done. Benton Cross took everything for granted. Benton Cross felt life owed him as many castles or countries or women as he desired. He had at least three castles that she knew of. And he—with his aristocratic good looks and uncounted wealth—seemed to belong anywhere he chose.

She glanced at her second companion, Mordecai Judd, a tall, handsome, dangerous-looking man of indeterminate race in his late thirties. Judd's shoulder-length braids and rough but colorful garments made him distinctly out-of-place here. She wondered if the pirate was having daydreams similar to her own. She wondered if he was tallying the worth of the furniture, the chandeliers, and the tapestries as his greedy gaze caressed them.

"Benton! What an unexpected surprise!"

The voice fell from the grand staircase that curved upward to the first floor of the palace. Hearing it, Cross stopped in the center of the hall and folded his hands at his waist.

"Atherton," was all he said.

The Regent, all smiles, continued to the bottom of the stair and crossed the hall to greet them, the heels of his gleaming black boots tapping confidently on the marble floor.

"Wonderful to see you, old friend," he told Cross, then turned to Daphne, taking her gloved hand and bowing over it with courtly grace. "Miss Bellanger, you are as lovely as ever."

His eyes flicked to the saber she wore sheathed at her waist, a reminder that she was also dangerous. She nodded in acknowledgement, her mouth curving in a smile. Atherton seemed to have no inkling of their reason for their visit. He was in for a rude surprise.

Cross finally spoke, turning to gesture at the skyraider. "May I introduce Captain Mordecai Judd, chief warlord of the Red Tong."

"Oh, yes," said Atherton smoothly, showing no surprise that Cross would have brought such a man into his home. "I know you, Captain. Your reputation precedes you." He smiled provocatively. "Back in the day, I hunted riffraff like you."

Judd inclined his head, making the shiny metal ferules in his braided locks sing like tiny bells. His dark eyes were lit with wry humor. "I trust we gave you a good chase, sir. We seem to have survived you all right."

Atherton's smile was pained. "Yes, well, I suppose you have. Please, why don't we retire to my study." He gestured over his shoulder at the staircase.

The party ascended to his first-floor study—as grand a room as Daphne had ever seen in any of the places she had lived with Benton Cross. Atherton, she understood, had had the place renovated the moment he was made Regent. She had to admit, he had exquisite taste.

The Regent crossed the thick, luxurious carpet to take a seat behind an enormous desk. One of the room's three fireplaces glowed at his back, larger than some of the places Daphne had lived in as a child. The mantlepiece was adorned with several flower arrangements that must have come from the hothouse they'd seen when they first arrived. Benton Cross did not like flowers.

"So, what brings you to Rotherwood?" the Regent asked, waving them to a scattering of silk-covered chairs and settees arranged artistically before the desk.

Cross elected to stand, as did Daphne. Judd seated himself upon a delicate white and gold Louis Quatorze chair and crossed his long, leather clad legs. He made such a ludicrous picture that Daphne had to stifle laughter, disguising it as a clearing of her throat. The only thing that would make the image more comical was a dainty cup of tea and tiny wedge of toast placed in the pirate's hands.

Cross glanced at her briefly, then turned his attention to Atherton. "I am here," he said, stripping off his gloves with tangible impatience, "simply because I am weary of getting news of your incompetence."

The affable smile dropped from Atherton's face. "I . . . I don't understand. To what do you refer?"

"I refer to the fact that another arms shipment has been confiscated by the Resistance. The third in two months. You assured me that your 'secret system' would guarantee the safety of this one. It did *not*. In addition, a scientist crucial to the Legion's continued success escaped from the Enfield facility. Far too easily, I might add."

Atherton frowned. "Yes, I am aware of all of this. However, just today, my men captured a key agent of the Resistance, Sir Henry Ramsay. I'm having him brought here as we speak."

Daphne raised an eyebrow at that news. She noted that even Cross was surprised. He prowled to the floor-to-ceiling windows on the southern side of the room and stared out over the rear of the estate. Daphne thought she heard him grinding his teeth.

"Ramsay?" he growled finally. "I should have known he'd throw his allegiance in with that lot."

"I have a special 'guest room' ready for him below," the Regent assured him. "I'll get him to tell us how to deal with Archangel and his pack of traitors."

Cross turned from the window and strode back to the center of the chamber, fixing Atherton with a glare that ought to have set him on fire. "You couldn't get a flea to bite a dog! You think Ramsay will talk for you? He's ex-SIS. He'll make you look a bigger fool than you already are."

Atherton, to his credit (and his detriment), rose to the insult. Literally. He stood, straightened his coat, and came out from behind his desk, fury darkening his face.

"I think it's time that you begin to respect the position you have bestowed upon me and allow me to run this country the way I see fit. England will prosper for you, I have no doubt."

"I have every doubt," countered Cross. "I think it's time you stepped down, Regent Atherton."

He punctuated the statement by grasping the hilt of Daphne's saber and ripping it from its scabbard. In a movement so swift she barely saw it, he slashed open Atherton's throat, nearly severing his head. He was dead before his body hit the floor.

Cross handed Daphne the bloodied sword, allowing the corpse a narrow-eyed look. "Your resignation is accepted, *old friend*."

Daphne's every instinct told her to run, but she stayed completely still, completely emotionless as she sheathed her saber. She glanced at Mordecai Judd, still seated in his dainty chair. He hadn't moved at all . . . except that his left hand was now draped across his stomach where it was in immediate reach of his pistol. His eyes were hooded and wary and fixed on Cross.

Cross spoke again, reclaiming Daphne's attention. "I am not letting Ramsay rot in some prison. Not when he can be of much use to us." He made an angry gesture at Judd. "Mordecai, when Sir Henry arrives, I want you to take charge of him. Your people have the most effective ways of acquiring information. Get what you can from him."

Judd rose languidly; Daphne half-expected him to stretch like a feral cat. "You can bank on it," he said.

Cross turned and started for the doors, then slanted a glance back over his shoulder at the bloody mess he'd made of Regent Atherton.

"And clean that up."

Daphne followed Cross from the room, affording Judd a look that was half commiseration, half mockery. He didn't notice her. He was too busy looking daggers at Cross's retreating back.

SEVEN -
WHAT LIES BENEATH

LONDON - ST. PANCRAS

THE SAD CALLS OF MOURNING DOVES TEMPERED THE HOPEFUL rising of the Sun. They seemed appropriate to the place—a massive cemetery on the fringes of the old city. Frost sparkled like a dew of diamonds on grass and stone and tree bough; the scene looked as if it had arrived by way of a painter's brush.

Brenden Winter, still wearing the guise of the good physician, Heywood Atkinson, made his way down one of the paved walkways in the oldest part of the cemetery. He passed by the mouth of an intersecting path and darted a glance in that direction.

Over there, perhaps 200 yards away, was a grave with his name on it. He never failed to think of it when he passed this way, though he never went anywhere near it. Not since—

"Top of the morning to you, Doctor!" called a cheery voice with a distinctly Scots brogue.

Winter pulled himself back from his memories and the cooing of the doves to see a slight, elfin young gentleman seated at the base of a stone angel that wept over a pair of graves, her wings shimmering with frost. His hair, which had overgrown his collar, stuck out at odd angles from his wool cap and a thin scruff of beard barely covered the bottom half of his face. He wore a long coat and a jaunty striped muffler against the cold and was munching on a piece of bread so fresh that Winter caught the warm, yeasty scent of it from where he stood.

"Having breakfast with the dead, Kenzie?" he inquired.

MacKenzie Graham stood and brushed the bread crumbs from his hands, offering a ready smile. "Oh, you'd be surprised what you can learn from the dead, Doc. So, tell me, then—how'd things go in town?"

"I got the message, but there were complications. A legion of them."

Kenzie joined Winter on the path, lowering his voice. "What? How could they know?"

"They did. Somehow. And they've arrested Sir Henry."

"Dear God, no!" breathed Kenzie. "What should we do? We must get him back!"

Winter turned and the two men began a circuitous ramble through the cemetery to its most overgrown corner.

"We do," Winter agreed. "But first we need to complete the mission at hand. The trap is set, and we cannot afford to let this opportunity slip through our fingers."

Even Kenzie was uncharacteristically silent as they made their way to their destination, a beautiful but weathered mausoleum labeled with the name *Thornton*. Set in the embrace of an ancient cedar, the tomb was large, but not nearly as ornate as the ones around it. Overgrown ivy and trailing roses obscured its lines; to all appearances it had fallen into disrepair. Its one remarkable feature was a stained-glass window set into the thick, oaken door that depicted the descent of the archangel Michael from heaven in clouds of crystalline glory.

With a casual glance to ensure that no one was anywhere nearby, Winter and Kenzie stepped into the shade and shelter offered by the low-hanging bows of the cedar and ascended the mausoleum's granite steps.

Winter still wore his codex ring. He used it now to dial in a code that would activate the lock on the mausoleum's iron-bound door. The door unlatched with a subtle *click* and opened silently inward. The two men stepped into a small chamber that was as unlike a tomb as could be imagined. The walls were of beaten brass, each large plate held in place with brass-capped rivets. A rainbow of light from the archangel window played across the softly gleaming surfaces. The chamber was completely empty.

Winter set a different configuration in the crown of his ring and pressed it into a small indentation on the rear wall of the brass room. There was a metallic ringing and a low-pitched hum, and the chamber lowered itself into the earth beneath the Thornton tomb. Lights set at four-foot intervals in the lift shaft flashed behind the stained-glass archangel, making him seem to move.

Mesmerized by the strobing patterns of light, Winter found himself thinking how many times he had been lowered into the earth alive and yet not alive. Dead to the world. Catchy old aphorism. He really was dead to the world, but it bothered him only that he was dead to Emily and Jonathan. It tormented him that they had watched an empty casket be lowered into a false grave, unknowing that he was yet alive.

Five people stood at my graveside, three men, a woman, and a child. Besides my weeping widow and my son, Artemus McDowell and Florian Buckingham were the only souls kind enough—knowing enough—to attend my 'funeral.' Father Carroll, faithful and dear, was the only clergyman who would have even considered presiding over it.

I stood in the shelter of a mausoleum, disguised, pretending to pray, instead watching my wife and child mourn my death. I hated to see Emily in 'widow's weeds,' hated to see Jon without his infectious smile. Most of all, I hated that the two men standing on either side of them knew I was still alive. Wounded, weak, but whole. My family and my priest had been told that my body had been too badly mutilated to allow them to see it. Florian had verified my death to them.

I wanted to run down the path crying out that I was still alive, that I had not assassinated the Queen of England, that I was no traitor, and that I would never leave them again. I would promise not to run away and hide as I knew other men had done. I would stay and fight with every asset and resource I possessed. Fight to take England back from the Legion.

Seeing my vibrant bride in raven's black and my son white-faced and in tears, I considered revealing to her and to Jon that I yet lived. I considered it seriously, desperately. I knew my Emily. She would insist on fighting by my side. As much as I desired that (oh, how I desired it), I could not have it. If I revealed myself to them, their lives would be endangered; with me 'dead,' they were no threat to the Legion, and it was no threat to them. Jonathan needed to be able to go to school, to grow to manhood as naturally as possible for a boy who now must be his mother's only partner in the world.

The wind shifted and the Reverend Carroll's words rolled up the hill to me.

"'I am convinced that neither death, nor life, nor angels, nor rulers, nor things present, nor things to come, nor powers, nor height, nor depth, nor anything else in all creation, will be able to separate us from the love of God in Christ Jesus our Lord," Father Carroll quoted.

I recognized the passage; it was in Romans, chapter eight. He moved next to the Lamentations of Jeremiah.

"Let us remember the words of the prophet Jeremiah: 'The steadfast love of the Lord never ceases, His mercies never come to an end; they are new every morning; great is His faithfulness.'"

He was trying to comfort my widow. Trying to let her know that regardless of what I was believed to have done—regardless of what I actually had *done in my service to the Crown—I was not lost.*

I loved him for that.

He did something that puzzled me, then. He raised his head, gazing up the hill toward where I knelt and said, in ringing tones: "Blessed are those who mourn, for they will be comforted.'"

Those were the words of Christ from the Beatitudes, and I knew of a certainty that they were for me. He was letting me know that my wife and son would someday rise from beneath their sorrow. I don't mean to imply that he sensed I was not gone; perhaps he intended the words of comfort for my supposedly disembodied spirit. Whatever his intent, I appreciated those words.

He looked back to the small gathering and said: "We have come here today to remember before God our brother, Brenden Winter; to give thanks for his life; to commend him to God our merciful redeemer and judge; to commit his body to be buried, and to comfort one another in our grief." Then he prayed: "God of all consolation, your Son Jesus Christ was moved to tears at the grave of Lazarus, his friend. Look with compassion on your children in their loss; give to troubled hearts the light of hope and strengthen in us the gift of faith, in Jesus Christ our Lord."

Five voices said the 'amen.' I heard Jonathan's over all others, ringing with resolve. Then the good Reverend Carroll tossed a handful of soil onto the empty casket and, with Artemus and Florian, escorted my family from the grave.

I vowed I would not visit it again.

The brass panel in front of Winter's face slid upward with a clatter, revealing the ample bi-level room beyond. In the lowered center of the chamber was a pool of light that shone down on a large round table with a map of London laid out upon it. Between the lift and the table was a horseshoe-shaped group of workbenches covered in a variety of electrical and chemical equipment that flashed lights and pulsed with energy or sprouted clear glass tubing that connected beakers filled with substances even Winter had no clue about.

This central section of the lab was sunken three feet below the gallery level on which Winter and Kenzie now stood. To both right and left were a series of workstation consoles, each with its own purpose—mechanical assembly, chemistry, communications. Farther along the right-hand wall was a floor to ceiling bookshelf containing volumes both philosophical and scientific. Winter had never understood the recent tendency to separate the two spheres of human life.

At the far end of the gallery was an alcove in which a light shone down on the Archangel armor. It was such a complete covering that even Winter had to remind himself there was no one inhabiting it. Sometimes it seemed a thing apart—a silent, watchful member of the team with a life of its own.

Clustered at the round table were two men and a young woman who'd obviously been engaged in a tense conversation. Having heard the lift box's door open, the three turned to the two men who'd entered, the eldest of the three—Artemus McDowell—wringing his hands in agitation.

"My God, Brenden! We just heard about Sir Henry. Our agent at the Tower said they've not brought him there, but taken him to the Regent at Rotherwood." Artemus paused and peered at Winter. "Are you quite all right, laddie?"

"I'm . . . yes, I'm fine. Gerrish . . . seemed suspicious of me, though I'm not sure why."

"Oh, I think he just enjoys being suspicious," said Kenzie, shoving his hands into the pockets of his breeches.

"Was there no chance of saving Sir Henry?" This came from Bobby Mortimer, the team's resident engineer and ordnance specialist. Bobby was an exceptional young man with a keen mind for engineering. He was especially good at making things explode—no surprise since he'd been born and raised in Woolwich, where his father worked in the Royal Ordnance Factory.

"There were too many of them, Bobby. Gerrish brought a whole squad with him. Sir Henry . . . Sir Henry sacrificed himself for the cause."

The young woman, Virginia Marie Gelsen, by name, stepped from behind Artemus, rubbing her arms as if she had caught a chill. She was dressed in clothes more suitable for a boy than a young woman just out of her teens, and wore them with an ease born of habit. The daughter of a peer, Ginny had rebelled against the attitudes and customs of her social class and, with the lax oversight of an indulgent father (who perhaps missed having a son), took up such unseemly activities as riding astride, fencing, and several forms of combat peculiar to Asia. She'd also developed a deep curiosity and passion for all things natural and had even dissected the occasional frog or snake using their cook's kitchen knives. In this, her father also indulged her, allowing her to be tutored in the subjects of botany, biology, and chemistry. Brenden Winter was bloody glad he had.

By the time she was fourteen, Ginny had struck out on her own academically, and earned herself a spot at the relatively young Catholic University of Ireland which, in less than forty years, had become one of the finest medical colleges in all of Britain. In another England, she might have become the first female surgeon in the nation. In this England, the assassination of Queen Victoria and the beginning of the Legion's brutal reign over the British Isles shunted her down a different path—the path of resistance.

She now used her talent for chemistry and biology to push back against the regime that had derailed her career and sent her mother and father into exile, along with many other members of the peerage. Ginny Gelsen, though still in her early twenties, was the undisputed mistress of the impressive forest of beakers and tubes that graced the lab.

"What do you think they'll do to him, sir?" she asked Winter solemnly.

"Uncertain." Seeing the anguished look on her face, Winter shook his head. "He knew the risks, Ginny. We all do. This is a deadly game we play. We've lost many good people—close friends, family. But the alternative is losing our souls and the soul of our nation. We can't give up the fight."

Ginny's expression stiffened, making her look far less vulnerable than she had the moment before. "I'd never suggest that we should, sir."

Artemus gestured toward the bank of tele-monitors that covered the communications workbench. "I'll have an intelligence update for you within the half-hour. I've got a half dozen operatives in the field."

Winter nodded, moving down the short flight of steps into the lab to remove his coat and set his satchel down on a desk he had claimed as his own. "Well then, I suggest we get back to work and continue with tonight's plans, assuming we receive confirmation."

Bobby and Ginny shared a glance, then nodded and went back to their stations in the upper gallery. Bobby was still unable to hide the profound limp that had resulted from a skyraider attack on his hometown. The pirates' target had been the royal munitions depot, but they'd unleashed terror on the whole of Woolwich when the inhabitants rose up to defend the factories. Bobby had sustained his life-changing wounds trying to save his family. His parents had been spared, but his little brother James had perished in the firefight.

The day Bobby discovered that the Legion had been using the skyraiders as their attack dogs in an attempt to acquire control of the Crown's source of munitions was the day he threw in his lot with the Resistance. His creativity, innovative ideas, and skill had brought him here, to Artemus McDowell's lab.

Winter was struck anew at the way disaster and tragedy, loss and upheaval, sundered old connections and created new ones. He was glad for every member of his team, yet unutterably regretful of the forces that had brought them here. He looked up now, as he worked to remove the parts of the Atkinson disguise that were easily reapplied and caught Artemus studying him a mite too intently. He was about to ask the older man what was wrong, when the communications console uttered a low beeping sound.

"Ah, that could be our confirmation now!" Artemus turned his inquisitive gaze away from Winter and trotted up the gallery steps to what he'd come to call the "telecom" and seated himself before the tele-monitors. Kenzie and Winter followed him.

Artemus slid his spectacles from the top of his head to the bridge of his nose and began twiddling dials and toggling switches. The beeping continued. Kenzie reached over the older man's shoulder toward a tele that was labeled Paris. Artemus slapped his hand away.

"Don't touch that, you silly boy! As if you knew how this all works . . . ."

"Happens, I do," Kenzie murmured to Winter, though he showed no offense at the scientist's rebuke.

Artemus now toggled several switches beneath the *Paris* tele himself (the very ones that Kenzie had reached for, Winter couldn't help but notice), and announced, "It's an encrypted transmission from Paris. Let me just dial in the proper cipher . . . ." He turned a dial that was a larger facsimile of the crown of Winter's codex ring.

The Paris tele-monitor lit up, displaying the live image of a round-faced woman of middle age with hair the color of winter wheat. As the image solidified, she smiled broadly, lips vibrant red against her white teeth and powdered cheeks.

"Artie, my handsome fellow! How lovely to see you!"

Artemus blushed, the back of his neck going red as a rose. Winter had never worked out whether his old colleague disliked this use of his pet name, but he did know that even their long association—which had begun when Artemus was the chief equipment and surveillance expert at the SIS—did not grant Winter such freedom.

"Well, Jackie, ahem, well—you too, of course."

Kenzie grinned and dug an elbow into Winter's ribs. Artemus was the only one of them who could get away with calling Madame Jacqueline "Jackie." Kenzie had tried it but once, and got a tongue-lashing that was no less potent for the fact that it was in French, of which the young man understood not a word. Winter, quite honestly, had no idea whether Artemus's use of the name was retaliation for her use of "Artie" or a return of her obvious affection. It was clear Kenzie thought it was the latter.

Winter gave the young Scotsman a raised eyebrow, then drew closer to the tele so that Jacqueline could see and hear him.

"What news do you have for us?"

"*Bonjour*, sir. The news is good. It seems the Legion has taken the bait. Ethan and Aiden were able to extract from their messenger the mission time, which appears to be at zero-two-hundred hours."

"Any estimate of how many soldiers we might expect?"

"*Non.* But I can tell you they have increased their effort to find Professor Tesla."

"Yes, so we've seen. I could only wish that Cross himself would be there tonight. Anything else?"

"*Oui.* I do not know if Monsieur Cross will be on the mission tonight. But I do know that he has returned to England."

"Thank you, Jacqueline. Tell the twins, *bon travail.* Good work."

"*Bien sûr.* Be safe, and God's speed, sir." Her eyes shifted to Artemus. "And you take care too, Artie, *mon chere.*" She blew him a kiss from her rose red lips, laughed, and ended the transmission.

Now Artemus's entire face had gone ruddy. But he was grinning like an unseasoned school boy. Winter suspected Kenzie was right about the scientist. He seemed smitten.

Kenzie leaned down and spoke into Artemus's ear. "Time to return to Earth, my little gigglemug."

Artemus turned in his seat and gave the younger man an arch look. "I'd suggest you keep that sauce-box closed, if you wish to remain on this planet, my lad. I'll not have a callow kid taunt me about matters he's too young to comprehend."

Kenzie straightened, threw back his head and laughed. "Oh, I comprehend being starstruck, y'old goat. I comprehend that just fine."

Winter, shaking his head, moved to where Ginny and Bobby sat at their respective workbenches. He leaned against the wall between the two and looked from one to the other.

"How do we stand on those special items for tonight?"

Ginny gave him a confident smile. "Dressed and ready to go."

"A right fit piece of engineering, if I do say so myself," Bobby added, kissing the tips of his fingers.

"Good to hear," Winter acknowledged. "But something tells me this won't be as easy as it seems."

EIGHT - WHAT LIES

LONDON OUTSKIRTS

HUNDREDS OF DERELICT TRAIN CARS WERE SCATTERED ACROSS THE abandoned yard like a giant child's forgotten toys. Occasionally, one or two might be taken away and others brought in. Some were inhabited by those who had no home elsewhere. Some would never move again, having been stripped of their wheels or had their wooden siding taken for firewood.

Among the jumble of cars wandered an old tramp in a long, filthy brown coat, every bit as battered and tattered as the train cars. He traced a relatively straight path down a string of a half-dozen boxcars, rubbing his hands together against the cold and seeking a place to roost. Eventually, he found a broken wooden crate and tipped it on end to make a stool upon which he sat. Reclining against the side of an abandoned boxcar, he reached into the pocket of his disreputable coat and removed a wizened apple, which he bit into with great relish. Just because something was a bit tatty on the outside didn't mean that what was inside wasn't good and useful.

He'd enjoyed perhaps half the apple when he heard the whine of engines. He raised his head and looked around, trying to discern where the sound was coming from. He settled on *up,* and lifted his eyes to the heavens, peering up at the clouds, whose fleecy forms were haloed with moonlight. With a suddenness that made him catch his breath in a hiss, the clouds roiled and writhed and two small skyships descended through them.

They'd no more than cleared the bellies of the clouds when each spat out a beam of light that lanced to the earth at the heart of the mechanical graveyard. Illumined by those spotlights, small objects began to pepper the ground, exploding to expel thick, oily smoke into which the skyships settled like oversized birds. Within seconds, orange-red tracers of energy lit the false fog from within, throwing the men who fired them into flickering silhouette.

Skyraiders. Though their bolts flew indiscriminately in all directions, there was no return fire at all.

Curious.

The tramp studied the situation but for a moment, then prudently sought cover. The boxcar he'd been leaning against would suffice, he decided. Holding onto his dilapidated bowler hat, he rolled beneath it to watch events unfold, all the while chewing on his apple.

From the billowing wall of smoke emerged a tall, dark man with long, intricately braided hair. Beside him was a man of similar height who was so lean and lanky that he looked as if he must subsist on air. Both of them were obviously rough men, used to fighting. Formidable. Too formidable to challenge, perhaps, armed as they were.

The one with the extraordinary hair called to the other, "Save your ammo, Jack. I want you to tear this place apart till you find that shipment."

The one called Jack responded by relaying the command to the other men. "You heard the captain! You lot, search that area." He gestured roughly half the group who'd followed him from the smokey fog to where the tramp crouched concealed beneath the boxcar. "The rest of you, come with me!"

The raiding party broke in two, then spread out even more, which immensely bettered the odds if a man were to challenge them. They fanned out among the derelict cars, shining electric torches into the gloomy interiors, and searching for this mysterious shipment of which their captain had spoken.

Two of the skyraiders wandered very near to the tramp's hiding place. He hesitated for only a moment before he rose up from under the boxcar, dealt one man a swift chop to the back of the neck, and took the other out just as deftly with a sweeping kick to his jaw. He disarmed both men without dislodging his bowler, then dragged their limp bodies beneath the boxcar, deciding to keep a couple of their weapons for himself and flinging the others away into the brush on the far side of the car.

When he emerged from hiding, he saw that the situation had altered. A remarkable figure in a dark, hooded coat and gleaming body armor was standing just at the end of the adjacent train car surveying the dissipating smoke through immense, glowing amber . . . well, not eyes, certainly, but lenses of some sort. As the tramp hesitated, considering his next move, the strange being turned its head and looked directly at him. He raised his empty hands (he'd secreted one weapon in the back of his belt and the other in his coat pocket) as if to proclaim his surrender. The being ignored him, turning away to murmur something so quietly, his words were indecipherable. Whether as a result of those words or mere coincidence, the space between the train cars was suddenly alight with a fresh volley of weapons fire.

The tramp did not look a gift horse in the mouth; he dropped and rolled back under the boxcar to watch.

Renewed gunfire pulled Mordecai Judd from the old passenger car he'd been inspecting and back toward the heart of the train yard. The men he'd assigned to Iron Rail Jack were being bombarded with energy blasts that rained on them from out of nowhere. Before he could isolate the direction and height of the bombardment, two of his men caught deadly bolts and fell.

Jack appeared from between a pair of passenger cars and jabbed a finger toward a boxcar some yards distant.

"There!" he cried. "Over there! Atop the car!"

Mordecai spun, following Jack's direction, and spied the moonlit silhouettes of perhaps a dozen men, all told, not just atop the car, but firing from beneath it, as well. The Resistance was here, after all.

"Damn it all to hell!" the skyraider captain growled, then quickly assembled his own men and ordered them to converge with Jack's.

"Take cover! Empty everything you've got into them, boys!" Mordecai roared.

His men obeyed instantly, firing from concealment and unleashing a barrage of blasts at the boxcar that lit it up like a firework barge. The enemy fighters were brightly illumined in the lurid light, making them excellent targets. Mordecai saw several fall from the roof. Parts of the car, and even men, caught fire, filling the night air with yet more smoke.

It took several minutes, but at last the enemy guns fell silent; no more lightning issued from the box car. After the sizzle and crackle of the deadly charges, the quiet was eerie. Mordecai's ears rang and his eyes saw traceries of light arcing against the darkness—an after-effect he was quite used to. Smoke eddied in the now-silent clearing, winding this way and that on errant currents.

After a moment of careful observation, Mordecai signaled his men forward, but urged caution. "Keep your eyes peeled, now, boys," he warned them, for his instincts told him something was not quite right. It seemed odd to him that the men atop the train car had not fired from a prone position, and that their fellows on the ground had not concealed themselves better. The Resistance may have started out as a motley mob of untrained commoners and nobles, but they were not known to be reckless or stupid.

Jack intercepted Mordecai as he made his way cautiously toward the boxcar.

"Nothin' like a clean win, eh, Cap? We made it look like Chinese New Year come early."

"Too easy," growled the captain. "It was too damned easy."

"We lost four men—well, two shot and two I can't find. You call that easy?"

Mordecai threw his lieutenant a dark look. "They sacrificed *all* their men. Why? What was the point of that?"

Jack shrugged. "I don't give a damn. They did it. And we'll have our property back in short order."

They'd reached the boxcar now. Not a living thing moved or breathed here. Mordecai muzzled his misgivings and shouted orders to his men.

"All of you! Get those doors open and get the crates out! Keep your eyes open for more of the Rezzies!"

The raiders swarmed the captured train car, shooting the lock from the bolted door and forcing the rusty door mechanism, which surrendered with a squawk of protest. As his men went about their work, Mordecai moved to stand over the nearest corpse, which lay face down on the cold ground.

Its arms and legs were splayed as if it had fallen from the roof of the boxcar. He prodded the body with his foot and was brought up short when it moved. He aimed his rifle at it and waited to see if it would move again. When it didn't, he rolled the body over with his foot.

He froze. The thing had no face. It wasn't just that half the face had been blown away, it was that what was left was not human. It was a brass mask that did not even have eyes in its empty sockets. In the ragged hole left by someone's lucky shot, was an assemblage of small clockwork gears, twisted and ruined.

This was never a man.

Panic rising in his gorge, Mordecai looked around and spied another body. He knelt beside it, ripping away the fabric of its shirt. This one, too, was a mere mannequin—a mechanical golem.

He leapt to his feet, screaming orders even as he bolted away from the train car. "Get out of there! Get out! Now! Go! *Go! GO!*"

Too late. He'd gone no more than ten feet when the boxcar exploded in an expanding ball of fire and debris. The shock wave sent Mordecai tumbling heels over head to skid painfully across the uneven ground until he fetched up against the wheels of a burnt-out Pullman car.

When he could orient himself and see again, he realized that many of his men had not been so lucky. Those who'd been inside the boxcar had simply been vaporized right along with it. He got shakily to his feet, struggling to assess how many men he'd lost and how many still lived. He saw Iron Rail Jack and a handful of other men about twelve or so yards away, also picking themselves up from the ground.

Mordecai turned toward them, opened his mouth to speak, and was driven to ground again by a new spate of gunfire that seemed to come from every direction at once. He hit the ground and rolled beneath the Pullman car. Heart beating out an alarm, he pulled a transmitter from his pocket and spoke urgently into it, his eyes on the lopsided battle.

"Get those ships down to the rendezvous spot and pick us up! We're under attack!"

He put his fingers to his mouth and sounded a sharp whistle. Any men who were not already fleeing toward the pickup point would hopefully hear it and take flight. If they didn't, it was on them.

Before he rolled from beneath the train car on its far side, Mordecai saw movement at the fringes of his vision. He twisted about to see the imposing figure of the Archangel stride out of concealment. Body armor glinting in the fitful light of the firefight, coat billowing around him, he seemed part of the smoke and darkness. Hatred roiled in Mordecai's breast and filled his head with flame. His trigger finger twitched and, for a second, he thought of shooting at the damned specter. It would likely not kill the man in his armor plating—if indeed he was a man—but it could very well result in Mordecai's capture or death.

He muzzled his rage, rolled from beneath the Pullman, and ran, dodging this way and that between the jumbled cars. Some yards away, he broke into an open area between a dilapidated roundhouse and the locomotive graveyard. His two ships had already drawn close to the ground, the doors of their gondolas open wide to receive the fleeing men; there were so few. Perhaps eight or ten. He saw that Jack had survived and stood by the gondola of the *Seahawk*, hastening the boarding. Seeing Mordecai, Jack nodded, then swung aboard himself.

Mordecai glanced back into the maze of abandoned cars and saw movement in the darkness. Archangel and his rabble were making their way toward the roundhouse. Snarling, the skyraider captain raced to his flagship, the *Condor*, and leapt aboard.

"Shall we away, Captain?" his pilot asked.

"A moment," Mordecai answered, his eyes on the broken wall of train cars.

"Sir?"

"I said wait! We'll go when I'm damn good and ready."

When he saw Archangel had a clear line of sight to him, though still too distant to get off a clean shot, he reached down and grasped the top of a large duffel bag that lay propped against the inner wall of the gondola next to the door. Heavy though it was, it took Mordecai only a single, rage-fueled tug to roll it out onto the ground.

"Away!" he ordered the pilot, then sent Archangel a satirical salute, capped off by a rude gesture. "Enjoy your present, you ugly bastard," he murmured.

He smiled grimly as the *Condor* rose skyward, watching as the Resistance fighters ran into the clearing, making straight for the duffel. Archangel halted them with a raised fist, then approached the bag cautiously, shining a light upon it that seemed to emanate from the palm of his hand. He was perhaps ten feet from it, when he abandoned caution and rushed to drop to his knees beside the bag.

Ah, yes. He'd seen it, then. Seen the dark stain of blood that soaked the duffel's dun fabric. The damned phantom drew his sword and sliced the bag open from top to bottom, revealing its contents—the bloody, much-abused corpse of Sir Henry Ramsay. Cradling the blood-matted head in his arms, Archangel lifted his glowing amber eyes to the skyraider's ship.

Now there's a picture.

Mordecai, smiling, offered Archangel an impudent salute, then closed the door of the gondola and sailed into the night sky.

NINE -
THRUST AND PARRY

REGENT'S PALACE - ROTHERWOOD

THE AIR WAS CHILL, BUT THE RISING SUN WARMED DAPHNE'S CHEEKS. She was warmed, too, from the heat of battle, excited by the song and flash of steel blades. Her breath came in sharp, cold bursts, soared out again in banners of steam. Her muscles responded to her direction with precision and force, her booted feet dancing over the pale stone of the broad terrace overlooking the rear of Rotherwood Manor.

Thrust, parry, spin, thrust. Dance.

Daphne Bellanger loved this exalted feeling. She laughed aloud. With a slash of her saber, she knocked aside her opponent's thrust, elated by the look of frustration on his face.

"Come now, my lord! Surely you can do better than that!"

His answer was a low-pitched growl as he leapt away and spun a full 180. He'd not quite completed the pivot when he flung his sword arm nearly behind him and made an off-balance lunge. Still laughing, Daphne batted his saber aside and went in herself for the "kill."

But Benton Cross was not as off-balance as he had seemed. He came in under her thrust and blocked her attack; their swords locked at the hilt, bringing them face to face.

Daphne's smile was wry and congratulatory at once. "I think someone's been practicing without me. Well done, Mr. Cross."

Cross, his eyes over-bright and his breathing harsh, leaned toward her as if for a kiss. Someone cleared their throat, shattering the moment. Daphne turned her head toward the French doors that opened onto the terrace, angry words clawing for escape. The intruder was the butler, Foster; in his hands was a silver tray containing two small towels, two cups, and a pot of tea wrapped in a third towel. There was also a small journal and a mechanical pencil.

"Thank you, Foster," Cross said, affording the butler a mere glance.

Daphne relaxed back a step, but Cross was not done with their fight. He thrust her away from him, forcing her to leap backward to stay on her feet. Then he lunged at her again. Anyone with less catlike reflexes than Daphne Bellanger would have been skewered. She batted his blade way and danced sideways.

"Sir," said the imperturbable Foster, "a Mr. Mordecai Judd and guest are here to see you."

"Fine. Bring them out." Cross said, then rounded on Daphne and flipped the sword into his left hand.

Bastard. He was trying to show her up. She focused all her attention on Cross, refusing to be diverted by the arrival of the two skyraiders, who stood by the doors, watching the duel. Though her back was to him, she heard Judd mutter something under his breath, then the damned idiot simply started walking toward the two combatants.

Cross must've thought her distracted, for he let out a great roar and lunged right at her. She was not distracted. She performed a swift disarm maneuver, catching his saber by the guard and flipping it into the air. She caught it with her free hand, spun and set the tip of her sword to Judd's throat, stopping him in his tracks.

Fortunately for him, his reflexes were also good. He suffered only the tiniest scratch. He gave her a slow, appreciative grin and raised his hands in surrender.

"You really like the swords, don't you?" he asked.

Daphne returned the grin. "They have a singular quality that I appreciate; they never need reloading or charging."

She turned then, and offered Cross his saber, hilt first. He accepted it with a wry smile.

"You must teach me that sometime, Daphne, my dear."

He crossed the terrace to a table upon which Foster had set his tray. The air was warming with the rising of the Sun, but the teapot was radiating steam. He picked up both hand towels and dabbed his forehead and neck with one, tossing the other to Daphne.

She caught it on the point of her sword and applied it to her own neck.

"Who's your friend?" she asked, flicking a glance at the gangly skyraider.

"This here's my lieutenant, Iron Rail Jack."

"Really. And how did you come by that moniker, Iron Rail Jack?"

The man favored her with an impertinent grin that made her skin crawl. "'Cause I'm long and thin as a rail and hard as iron . . . ma'am."

Daphne turned away and moved to the tea table.

"So, Captain," said Cross, pouring tea into his cup, "did you recover the shipment? Did you find Tesla?"

"Well, that's what we've come to report on. Things didn't go as we'd expected. Turns out, it was a trap. I doubt the arms were ever there at all."

"Aye. We barely got out of there alive," added Iron Rail Jack.

Cross set down the tea pot with so much force Daphne half-expected it to shatter, metal or no.

"So, let me understand this. You did *not* get the crates of arms. You did *not* find Tesla and you come here empty-handed?"

Judd stepped forward, anger smoldering in his dark eyes. "They were waiting for us. I lost over half my crew."

"They," said Cross.

"Who'd you expect? The damned Resistance . . . and Archangel."

"Archangel," repeated Cross, his voice filled with loathing. "London is becoming quite the problem. I sometimes think I should just go in there and level the entire city. Alas, that would be . . . counter-productive."

Daphne reached out to touch his shoulder soothingly. He gave her an unreadable glance, then picked up his tea cup and took a sip.

"Well, what now?" asked Judd.

"I have plans," Cross told him, "to put a warlord in place to command each of our conquered cities. They will be my eyes and ears."

Daphne did not miss the subtle change of expression on Judd's handsome face. No doubt the leader of the Red Tong would relish the opportunity to be the eyes and ears of a man like Benton Cross.

"But until then," Cross went on, "we must crush this Archangel and his cadre of insurgents. If we don't, this current of independence and rebellion will spill over to other countries. If even the most timid of people think that resistance is occasionally successful, they will band together and attempt it themselves."

"So, bombing is out of the question?"

Daphne thought Judd seemed disappointed.

Cross chuckled and shook his head. "Mordecai, Mordecai. Would you rid a ship of rats by burning the ship to the waterline? Naturally not, for they will simply swim to another ship. That is the nature of rats." Cross turned and handed his sword to Daphne, then picked up the journal and pencil from the tea tray. "The only effective way of killing every last one of them is cell by cell and one by one."

Judd folded his arms across his muscular chest. "And how do you propose to do that?"

Cross didn't answer right away. Instead he jotted notes in his journal. At length, he spoke again.

"Our dear, departed Dr. Tesla was the catalyst necessary to accelerate this plan. However, I believe we are far enough along that we should be able to figure out many of the problems inherent in the process." He paused contemplatively then added, "Still, it would be to our advantage to have the good doctor back in the Legion fold."

Judd shook his head, the tiny metal ferules binding his hair making a shimmering veil of sound. "I still don't understand exactly what you have in mind, Cross."

Cross began a slow meander around the two skyraiders, tapping his mechanical pencil against the pages of the journal. A patronizing smile played at the corners of his mouth.

"This doesn't surprise me, Mordecai. Let me ask you this: what would a world ruled by fear look like?"

"Brilliant!" said Iron Rail Jack enthusiastically.

"I don't follow," said Judd, literally trying to follow Cross's movements as he circled the terrace.

"Allow me to illustrate."

As Cross passed behind Iron Rail Jack, he clicked a button on the top of the mechanical pencil. A narrow metal spike sprang from the tip.

Before Daphne could do more than suck in a breath, he had driven the spike into Jack's skinny neck.

Ten - At All Costs

LONDON

D R. HEYWOOD ATKINSON STEERED HIS COMPANION THROUGH THE bustle of a London morning, eyes scanning for too-curious observers. His companion, Nikola Tesla, was wearing a large greatcoat that disguised his slender frame, and a large, floppy hat that had not been in fashion for a decade or more and then only among rural clergymen.

"I must protest," the professor said now. "I really don't see the need for this absurd disguise, Doctor."

"Trust me, professor, it's for your own safety."

"Really? If it was safety the Resistance was worried about, then why did Archangel have a man of medicine escort me, rather than a real bodyguard?" He halted and gave his escort an apologetic look. "I'm so sorry, Dr. Atkinson. I didn't mean to imply that you are incapable of defending me, should the need arise. I hope I didn't offend."

Winter/Atkinson smiled. "No offense taken, professor." He took hold of the scientist's arm and resumed their journey.

"Again, who exactly are we meeting with?" asked Tesla. "You were rather vague in your initial description of the gentleman."

Winter answered without answering. "He is a man of renowned intelligence and powers of observation whom I have asked to help us determine what the Legion plans to do with your research."

"Which tells me nothing at all," groused Tesla, adjusting the brim of his hat.

"Here we are," said Winter, stopping their forward progress.

They had arrived at a rather nondescript brownstone building, situated mid-block on a cobbled way. Winter checked the address. Yes, this was indeed the place: 221B Baker Street, home of the celebrated sleuth, Sherlock Holmes—a figure both prized and disparaged by the short-lived Scotland Yard.

Winter rang the bell, which was swiftly answered by a lovely older woman whose erect posture and bright eyes suggested boundless energy.

"Yes?" she said.

Winter tipped his hat. "Drs. Heywood Atkinson and Nigel Turnbull to see Mr. Holmes."

"Oh, yes sir. He's expecting you. Please, come in."

She led them up to the first floor suite of rooms occupied by the detective and delivered them into a spacious chamber that was as much museum, laboratory and library as it was parlor. There were two desks and a worktable covered with books, papers, test tubes, devices the purpose of which Winter could only guess at, and other oddities, including animal skulls.

Ginny, he thought, *would love it here.*

"Drs. Atkinson and Turnbull are here to see you, gentlemen."

A brown-haired man Winter judged to be in his mid-thirties folded the newspaper he'd been reading, all but leapt from his overstuffed chair, and hastened to greet them.

"Mrs. Hudson, could you kindly bring our guests some tea?" he asked.

"Very good, Doctor. I'll be just a moment, the kettle's already on the stove."

The young doctor turned back to Winter, taking his hand and shaking it energetically. "I'm Dr. John Watson. It's so good to finally meet you, Dr. Atkinson. We have several mutual acquaintances." He turned to Tesla then and said, "Dr. Turnbull, is it?"

"No, Watson. This is not Nigel Turnbull. It is Professor Nikola Tesla."

This quiet observation of fact came from a second gentleman who was standing by the window with a peculiar alabaster ball in one hand and a magnifying glass in the other. In response to that observation, John Watson's face registered surprise bordering on epiphany.

"My God! Dr. Tesla!" He shook the scientist's hand with even more enthusiasm than he had Atkinson's. "Your reputation precedes you, sir! May I introduce you both to Mr. Sherlock Holmes?"

The man at the window set down his ball and glass and turned to his visitors. Winter took him to be in his late forties or early fifties. He had hawkish features, pale, keen eyes, a distinguished, almost haughty bearing, and the beginnings of a beard. Winter had never met him, but he looked somehow familiar.

"Gentlemen, it was good of you to come. I'm pleased you sought my assistance. With things as they are, my work for the government has come to rather a standstill." He paused, his gaze unwaveringly on Winter, then said, "Watson, be so kind as to take Dr. Tesla to our cloak room so he can rid himself of that 'disguise.' He looks like a provincial cleric . . . who has just awakened after having slept for twenty years or so."

Watson smiled affably. "Absolutely, Holmes. Dr. Tesla, if you will follow me, I will show you where you can hang your things."

The two men left the room through the door closest to the entrance of the suite.

"So, Doctor," Holmes said, gesturing Winter to a chair near the fire. "I am surprised our paths have not crossed more than they already have."

Winter removed his own hat and coat and lay them on the arm of the chair before seating himself. "Already have? How is that, Mr. Holmes? I certainly don't remember meeting you, and I think I should."

Holmes did not sit, but wandered the room, touching this or that object, yet rarely taking his eyes from Winter. It was singularly unnerving.

"You may not know me," said the detective, "but I certainly do know you. And now, seeing you in this intimate setting, I see my assessment is well-founded. Your eyes tell me you are a man who has lost everything. Your hands are a bit too rough and your knuckles too callused for a man of medicine. They try to tell me that you are a farmer . . . or a warrior. Your physique is athletic and toned. Hardly the physique of someone who sits behind a desk and prescribes remedies all day. Your bearing and gait tell me you are—or were—a military man. Your footsteps are oddly silent and suggest you have practiced stealth."

Holmes had circled Winter's chair and returned to the window at which he'd been standing when they'd first seen him. Winter stifled a shiver of unease. Where was this going?

"There are some intriguing anomalies, too," Holmes said.

"Anomalies?" Winter repeated, trying to hide his disquiet. He turned his head slightly, so as to regard the older man out of the tail of his eye.

"Mmm, yes. Despite your workman's hands, your skin is fair and untouched by the sun. If you *were* a farmer, as your hands suggest, you would have a darker complexion. I favor the theory that you were—that you *are*—a warrior. And a good one, as you are still alive above the age of thirty. And finally . . . ." He paused, toying with something on the desk nearest the window. "Your reflexes—"

In a fraction of a second, Holmes had hefted the alabaster ball and pitched it at Winter's head. With equally lightning speed, Winter snatched it out of the air, just shy of his left ear.

"—are simply extraordinary, Dr. Atkinson. Or should I call you Lieutenant Colonel Brenden Winter?"

Winter froze in his chair, his focus entirely on Holmes now. Still, he kept his expression neutral, only lifting an eyebrow in response. He set the ball carefully on the tea table that reposed before the hearth.

"You have me at a disadvantage, Mr. Holmes," he said.

Holmes ignored the comment. "Brenden Winter is allegedly dead. Do you, perhaps, go by . . . Archangel?"

Now, Winter laid a hand on the pocket of his coat, feeling the solid shape of the pistol concealed in it. "My identity is known to only a select few. If the truth should ever get out, it would endanger my family, my friends, and my mission."

The detective's angular face lit in a smile. "Oh, please don't worry, sir. Your secret is quite safe with me. We're warriors in the same battle, you see, and fighting for the same cause."

"How can you possibly know this? What makes you think—?"

"The last time I saw you, Lieutenant Colonel, you were busy battling an aggressive and well-armed group of miscreants who seemed intent on ransacking a boxcar that I knew to be empty." He made a wry face. "Well, at least it was empty of what they clearly expected to find there. You blew them up, I believe. Or so the fireball I saw as I left the area suggested. You saw me there, as clearly as I saw you. I must say, I was surprised you didn't challenge me."

Of course. The old vagrant. Winter shook his head. "I must say, you clean up nicely, Mr. Holmes."

Holmes's smile deepened.

Watson and Tesla reentered the room then, just in time to admit Mrs. Hudson with her overburdened tea tray. There was not only tea, but crumpets, scones, and pots of jam, clotted cream, and lemon curd. She bustled to the hearthside tea table, delivered the refreshments, then turned and headed immediately for the door. She must be well-used to her tenants having secretive meetings and knew when her absence was required.

"Thank you, Mrs. Hudson," Watson called out to her. "It looks divine, as always."

Winter caught the woman's smile as she slipped out through the parlor door, closing it behind her.

Dropping into the chair opposite Winter's, Holmes rubbed his hands together like a child whose eyes have just fallen upon his birthday cake.

"Excellent. Have a seat, gentlemen. Before I share my findings with you, may I ask you, Dr. Tesla, what exactly was the nature of your new line of experimentation?"

The scientist perched, frowning, on the edge of an overstuffed chair. "You are obviously familiar with my theories of alternating current. It is what allows us to have electricity flowing throughout our world and powering our devices."

"Naturally," agreed Holmes. "Any schoolchild knows that it is your invention of the electrical filament that allows them to read tales of adventure late into the night and understands that it is in your honor that electricity is measured in teslas. And I know not one person of business who would not rather have your ingenious light globes illuminating their offices than the more dangerous gaslights."

Tesla blushed like a bride at the acknowledgment of his considerable achievements. "I appreciate your kind words, Mr. Holmes. As you say, I have, over the past three years, started on a new area of experimentation." He edged even farther forward on his chair, putting himself in jeopardy of slipping completely out of it. "What if," he said, his narrow face flushed with obvious excitement. "What if we could harness power from the Ether all around us? Use the Earth itself—indeed, use the stuff of the cosmos—as a power source?"

Winter turned to look at the scientist. "What is this . . . Ether?"

Tesla gave him an assessing look, then said, "I will try to make it simple. Ether is a sort of invisible or, perhaps, dark energy that surrounds us no matter where we are. It controls many elements of our existence, such as life, light, magnetism, and fire. Even electricity could not exist without the Ether. Nothing can. I have come up with a way that we can employ the pulsing currents of magnetism that flow through the Ether and utilize them. By harnessing this Ether, we could broadcast energy around the entire world without the use of wires, we could speed the healing of wounds and be the masters of amazing regenerative powers."

Holmes's face was opaque, but his body suggested tightly controlled energy. Perhaps, thought Winter, they could use Sherlock Holmes to power the world.

"Regenerative powers, Dr. Tesla? Regenerative powers that could save a dying man or even return a newly dead man to life?"

Tesla darted a glance at his three companions. "I . . . that is. Yes. That is precisely what I speak of."

"How close are you to testing this, professor?" Holmes asked.

Tesla blinked. "Testing? My testing was completed more than a year ago; this is now established, practical science."

John Watson gasped. "Amazing!"

Winter felt as if a cold, steel spike had been driven through his heart. This was madness.

Holmes was silent for a long moment, then asked, "Have any of you heard of or read a novel by Mary Wollstonecraft Shelley entitled *Frankenstein: The Modern Prometheus*?"

Winter and Watson nodded; Tesla said, "Of course."

"It seems that in the case of Mrs. Shelley's novel, art imitated life. In 1802, a Scottish scientist by the name of Malcolm Bullock began experimenting with dead tissue. Through much trial and error, he became rather successful in his quest for 'new-life,' as he called it. However, once the locals found out about these bizarre goings-on, they formed a lynch mob and beat Bullock to death. News of his demise came and went without much notice, except in scientific circles. The stories of his macabre exploits became sort of a Holy Grail, if you will, for every young medical student. This story had circulated for years by the time Mary Shelley wrote her novel. It's conceivable that she knew of Bullock's experiments—possibly through her connections to Lord Byron's physician friend, Dr. John Polidori. In any event, she shone her literary light upon it, made quite the name for herself, and expanded the imaginations of her readers."

Winter began to see a horrific connection to Tesla's work. "You suggest that the Legion might have also become aware of Bullock's experiments?"

"My sources tell me that about five years ago, a certain German doctor became quite obsessed with this story and actually tracked down a folio of Bullock's papers."

Tesla clutched the arms of his chair as if afraid it might throw him like an unruly horse. "Excuse me, Mr. Holmes, was this doctor's name von Brant? I heard that name frequently while I was captive."

Holmes turned to regard the scientist with a frown. "That name has been bandied about, though none of my sources was certain of the man's identity. Apparently, he goes by a number of aliases. Supposedly, this German was imprisoned for a time because of his experiments, but he escaped and is now allegedly here in England continuing his operations. Word has it, in the scientific community, that he has been working with cadavers, and has been somewhat successful in reanimating them. I say 'somewhat' because his 'reanimates' apparently have a relatively short life span—say, two or three years. However, gentlemen, I fear that the Legion may be on the verge of taking these nightmarish experiments to a much higher level."

Tesla had paled so much Winter feared he'd swoon. "My work with the Ether," he murmured through stiff lips.

Holmes nodded solemnly. "With this new Ether technology that Dr. Tesla has discovered, the Legion potentially has the ability to improve upon their existing experiments and create an endless supply of undead operatives, which could possibly live forever."

Winter was appalled by the thought. "A virtual army of the walking dead."

"Ghastly!" exclaimed Watson.

Tesla's expression changed with lightning speed to one of barely controlled fury. "What do you propose Mr. Holmes? What can we do?"

"You need to locate the laboratory where these aberrations are to be created. Such a facility surely exists by now. It must be destroyed utterly, along with all of this research. It must be buried, gentlemen. Once and for all."

"It *does* exist, Mr. Holmes," said Tesla, his voice trembling. "I have seen it. I was imprisoned there and barely managed to escape it. May I hope you propose to embark on this endeavor with us?"

Holmes stood as if unable to sit still any longer. He moved to stand at the hearth. "Unfortunately, no. I have been on the trail of another criminal mind who, if not stopped, will throw his seemingly bottomless resources in with the Legion. This he has threatened to do repeatedly."

"Who is he?" asked Winter.

Holmes shook his head. "I am uncertain. Which makes him even more dangerous. He simply signs his threats with the letter 'M.'" He turned abruptly to face Winter. "Dr. Atkinson, if you can, you must contact the Archangel and ask for his assistance in spearheading this operation."

"Do you think that he will want to take on such a task?" asked Tesla. "Remember, gentlemen, I was there in that horrible place. It is immense, heavily guarded, and even I have have only ever seen one laboratory, the cell I was imprisoned in, and the corridors that connected them. In order to destroy this regeneration lab, Archangel must first find it."

"Oh, yes," said Winter, his voice tight with purpose. "Archangel will doubtless be willing—even eager—to take this on. And with him, every man in the Resistance. For if we don't stop Benton Cross and the Legion now, this black science will allow him to become a virtual god."

"Such an evil the world has never seen," murmured Tesla, leaning back in his chair.

"The first thing you must do, sir," Holmes told Winter, "is to get Dr. Tesla out of the city, although out of the country would be better. The Legion will be doing everything in its power to recapture him for his knowledge and expertise. You must prevent this at all costs."

At all costs, Winter thought. His gaze was on Nikola Tesla, but in his mind's eye he saw the bloodied, tortured body of Henry Ramsay. How many more of them would have to pay "all costs" before this was over?

Eleven - Von Brant

ENFIELD

VON BRANT'S LABORATORY HAD MADE DAPHNE NERVOUS FROM the first moment she'd seen it. It was a cavernous room—having once been a factory floor—that was now full of a confusing array of electrical apparatuses, chemistry paraphernalia, and inexplicable machinery that she did not understand. Perhaps that was what disturbed her about the place—her lack of comprehension of any of it. It was *terra incognita*—unknown and therefore unsettling. It was rendered more disturbing today by the fact that there was a sheet-draped body on one of the metal tables near the center of the room.

Daphne stood staring at the table and the mysterious apparatus that loomed above it, rubbing her arms as if the chill she felt was a physical one. She heard a door open behind her and stopped the reflexive motion. It would not do for Benton Cross to believe she was skittish. She could not chance him losing respect for her.

"I have given Doctor von Brant this portion of the facility to conduct his experiments," Cross was telling his companion, Mordecai Judd. "If his work progresses at its current pace, this will be just one of many factories manufacturing an army of loyal soldiers. Ah, Daphne! Here you are!"

She turned to the two men with a smile. "You requested my presence. Where else would I be?"

Judd was regarding the Legion Warlord with frowning puzzlement. "Soldiers? How d'you manufacture soldiers?"

Cross didn't answer. He'd turned to greet the fourth person in the room—Dr. Viktor von Brant—who had appeared from around the bulk of one of the lab's machines. Von Brant was a frail man in his mid-sixties though he looked years older. His face was deeply lined and his thinning hair had gone iron gray. Daphne understood that he'd lived a hard life—part of which he'd spent in prison.

"Ah!" he said, seeing Cross and Judd. "You are right on time. Excellent." He gave Judd a particularly searching look. "And you are?"

"Mordecai. Mordecai Judd." The big skyraider extended his hand.

"You seem familiar to me, though I can't place where we might have met. I am Dr. Viktor von Brant. Forgive me, but I don't shake hands."

Judd pulled his hand back with a scowl that clearly telegraphed his affront. Von Brant seemed not to notice.

"Are you ready for the big revelation?" Cross asked. He was unable to keep the excitement from his eyes. It allowed Daphne a rare glimpse of what he might have been like as a boy, enraptured by some new toy.

The scientist nodded, smiling, his own excitement evident. "I am. Please, for your own safety, stand up there, away from the table." He waved them to a low gallery that rose about three feet above the lab floor and was roughly eight feet from the mysterious table.

Daphne was only too happy to comply. The further she was from that table, the better. She was relieved she would not have to decide what to do if von Brant invited them to gather around the damned thing. From the added height they could see quite well whatever it was the old man had to show them. Daphne caught herself just shy of glancing about to locate the nearest exit and forced herself to face the table.

Once she, Cross, and Judd had gone up the four steps to the gallery and arranged themselves along its rail, von Brant moved to the table and with a grand gesture, pulled the sheet away from its contents. As Daphne had suspected, it was a body. More specifically, it was the body of Iron Rail Jack.

Next to her, Mordecai Judd went stiff and cried out. "Jack!" He did a most unexpected thing, then; he crossed himself like a child at mass, murmuring words she couldn't hear. Then he fixed the scientist with a violent look that was equal parts dread and fury and demanded, "What are you going to do to him?"

Von Brant smiled. That smile was one of the most vile and terrifying things Daphne Bellanger had ever seen. She concealed a shiver and tried to keep her eyes steadily on a point just over von Brant's shoulder.

"Watch, Mr. Judd, and you shall see a miracle," promised the old scientist.

He turned the dead man's head so that his audience could clearly see a small metal disc—perhaps the size of a man's thumbnail—embedded in the dead man's temple.

"These small discs," he continued, indicating that there was a matching one on the opposite temple, "are battery units, which I have implanted into this man's skull. They are attached directly to his brain and will serve as a 'receptor' for an electrical current. Not only will they revive his body, but they will store this energy and feed the brain the necessary impulses to keep him alive for, oh, several years, I should think. Of course, he will need periodic charging, from time-to-time." He chuckled as if he found the idea of charging a human being amusing.

Mordecai Judd did not seem to find it amusing. "You . . . you've resurrected him? What, like Christ revived Lazarus?"

Von Brant nodded. "Indeed. A miracle, as I said."

Judd mumbled something of which Daphne heard only the word "God," then asked "Why such a short time?"

"Ah, because, our batteries are electrical and by no means permanent. They simply . . . burn out."

"Well then, why not simply give him new ones?"

"Because," said the scientist patiently, as if he were talking to a child, "when they burn out, they destroy brain tissue. Enough to affect viability. Thanks to Dr. Tesla, we are working on a new Ether-based implant, which could give the recipient essentially eternal life. As long as the body survived physical destruction, the person reanimated with these Ether units would remain animated." He frowned. "However, Dr. Tesla has, em, liberated himself."

"Eternal life?" repeated Judd. He sounded dazed.

Cross ignored him. "Never fear, Viktor. We will have Tesla and his notes back soon enough. Won't we, Daphne, my dear?"

She nodded in agreement, unable to pull her eyes away from the disc on the side of the skyraider's head.

"And now, Doctor," said Cross, "please continue your demonstration."

"Ah! Yes! Yes!"

Von Brant lifted a metal helmet from a shelf at the head of the table and placed it over the cadaver's head, aligning two metal pins on the sides of the dome with the discs embedded in the dead man's temples. That done, he began to run around the laboratory with the excitement of a child on Christmas morning, throwing levers and pressing buttons that caused the machinery around the table to come online with the flashing of lights and the sound of turbines kicking in. The apparatus over the table was bathed in an increasingly vivid blue glow.

Whatever von Brant was doing, it was drawing enough power to cause the overhead lights to flicker and dim. Daphne cringed. Her mother had once told her that the flickering of lights was evidence that demons were present. The idea had frightened her as a child. As an adult, she'd learned to scoff at it. Now, at this moment, watching lights flash and flicker and feeling the pulse of electricity raising the hair all over her body, she doubted that learning.

Von Brant did a full turn in the middle of his lab, seeming satisfied that everything was performing as it should. Then he moved to a control panel closer to the table and donned a pair of goggles with darkened lenses.

"Lady and gentlemen," he shouted over the sound of machinery, "please, shield your eyes!" He paused, perhaps to allow them time to do this, or perhaps for dramatic effect, then announced: "I give you the miracle of life!"

He threw a red-handled switch on the control panel causing arcs of electrical energy to stream down from the apparatus above the bed to the metal helmet that covered Iron Rail Jack's skull. The blue glow that had haloed the device was now channeled into two concentrated beams, which flow directly into the receptors on the side of Jack's temples.

Though the body was strapped down, it began to writhe, to jump and jitter like a marionette in a windstorm. Von Brant, still standing at the control panel, eyes riveted on a timer, began a countdown in German.

"Drei! Zwei! Eins!" he cried at the end of the recitation, and pulled the red-handled switch to the off position.

As suddenly as they had begun, the arcs of electricity and the two blue beams of light vanished, the generators wound down, and the electric tingle ebbed. The overhead lights flickered one last time, then returned to their normal brightness.

Daphne, who'd watched the play of light with half-closed eyes, was fairly certain there were still demons in the room. She found she was grinding her teeth and willed her jaw to relax. She smelt smoke and realized that the sheets that had covered the body were smoldering in places.

Von Brant moved to the table and pulled the singed sheet away. "Please, someone help me."

Judd moved to assist the doctor, while Daphne, repulsed, stayed where she was as if rooted to the gallery floor. She was relieved that Cross had not moved either, though she was certain it was for reasons bearing no resemblance to her own.

Von Brant began to unfasten the straps that held the body in place. "Help me with these straps," he told Judd.

It took the two men mere moments to free the body of the webbing. Von Brant moved to the head of the table and removed the helmet, placing it back on its stand.

Mordecai Judd was staring at the face of his lieutenant, looking—for the first time since Daphne had known him—completely unmanned. She didn't wonder at this; Iron Rail Jack's face looked withered and gray. Desiccated. Nor was he moving.

"What should we do?" asked Judd, leaning over the body.

Von Brant grasped his shoulders and physically pulled him back. "Move away. We must be patient . . . and careful."

A grim silence filled the laboratory. The only faint sounds Daphne could hear were the breathing of the living and the tic-tic-tic of cooling metal. She realized she had taken a death grip on the gallery rail and forced her hands open, crossing her arms over her breasts in an attempt to look impatient or bored.

The silence lingered long enough to cause even Benton Cross concern. He'd opened his mouth to say something when Iron Rail Jack sat bolt upright and uttered the scream of a tortured soul. The scream echoed from the rafters, the brick walls, and the high, clerestory windows.

Daphne could not help herself; she covered her ears and closed her eyes. A moment passed and she felt a light touch on her cheek. She dared open her eyes and found herself looking up into Benton Cross's amused face.

"Are you quite all right, my dear?" he asked.

She lowered her hands from her ears and twisted her face into a disdainful snarl. "I'm fine," she snapped. "Has the damn fool stopped shrieking? I swear I can't tell. I think I'm deaf."

"Come see," Cross said and led her from the gallery down to the laboratory floor. It took every ounce of her will not to resist him.

Von Brant was waving them toward the table. "It's safe now. Come. Come."

The scientist moved to the table and helped Iron Rail Jack to swing his legs over the side of the table. By the time Daphne and Cross reached the table, the man (the resurrected man) was standing, albeit on wobbly legs. He looked up as they neared, his eyes falling on Cross.

"You . . . you killed me," he said, his voice sounding vague and puzzled. He turned to his captain. "He killed me, Mordecai. He did. So, how am I alive? Or are we all dead?"

Judd shook his head, metal fittings jingling. "No, Jack, no one here is dead. You are very much alive."

"Oh, it gets better," said Cross.

Before she could guess his intent, he reached down, pulled her pistol from her holster, took quick aim, and shot Jack in the chest.

Judd let out a roar of rage and Jack screamed. He fell back against the table from the impact of the charge, but then put a shaking hand to his chest . . . where there was no sign of bleeding. The wound— which all could see clearly through the man's torn shirt—was already closing up.

Iron Rail Jack stuck a finger through the hole in his shirt. "What the hell?" He felt his chest, then looked up at those gathered around him and grinned. "Oh, now, this is different."

Benton Cross stepped over to the newly reanimated man and put a hand on his shoulder. "My friend, you have joined the ranks of a whole new breed . . . and I have a very special job for you."

Jack's grin widened and took on a manic twist. Daphne was certain, then, that the demons in Dr. von Brant's lab had never left, but only found a new place of residence.

Twelve - Lazarus

LONDON

WE WILL NEED TO GET YOU ON A TRANSPORT TONIGHT, Doctor." Winter's eyes were watchful as he guided Nikola Tesla through the lamplit London streets on their way back to the safe house in which they'd hidden the scientist. Any passer-by could potentially be a member of the Legion or one of their witting or unwitting informants.

Tesla had been a guest at Archangel's underground headquarters since the early twilit hours of the morning, going over his notes with Artemus McDowell and sharing many of his scientific insights with the team. As much as Artemus and company would love to keep their foreign colleague around, Winter knew that would be far too dangerous—to the Resistance cause and to Tesla, himself.

"Where are you sending me?" Tesla asked as they turned into the narrow alley that led, eventually, to the safe house.

"The safest place for now would be Geneva. It is a favorite of wealthy foreign recluses; you will merely be one more—and possibly one of the least eccentric. We have agents there that can house you in utter safety. How soon can you be packed and ready?"

"I can be ready almost immediately. After all, I have but the clothing you purchased for me and my folio—which I thank you for copying rather than making me leave it with Mr. McDowell."

"Good. When we get to the house, I'll contact McDowell and ask him to send a driver."

As they made their way past a series of sad-looking row houses, of which the Resistance safe house was an anonymous member, Tesla spoke again. "I want to thank you, Doctor, for everything that you and your people—and, of course, the Archangel— have done for me. I will be eternally grateful."

Winter didn't answer. His eyes were on the porch of the narrow building that served to safely hide those who had need to be safely hidden. There was no light in the window of the parlor. In fact, there was no light anywhere in the building that was visible to the outside. He stopped walking and grasped Tesla's upper arm.

"What is it?" the scientist asked. "What's wrong?"

"There is no sentry," murmured Winter. "There should be a vagrant pretending to sleep in the shelter of the front steps. He's gone. And all the lights are off. This doesn't look right."

He reached into his coat pocket and removed a small black device the size of a ha'penny. He put his hand on Tesla's shoulder and whispered into his ear. "Stay here, don't make a sound and stay out of sight. I'll signal you if it's safe to come in."

Tesla slanted a worried glance at the safe house. "Be careful, Doctor."

Winter patted the other man's back, using the motion to push the little device further beneath the collar of his coat. Then he pulled a pistol from another pocket and made his way stealthily towards the front porch of the safe house. At the bottom of the steps, he could clearly see that the door was ajar. Every sense heightened, he padded up the steps, put his ear to the door and listened. He heard exactly nothing.

Taking a deep breath, he pushed the door inward. It stopped; something was blocking it from opening all the way. Winter looked down, knowing what he would see; the body of one of the safe house's four guards lay across the inward path of the door. In the wan light of the half-moon, Winter could see the dark stain of blood that had pooled beneath the man. He was quite obviously dead.

Glancing back over his shoulder at Tesla, Winter pushed the door hard enough to shove the body farther into the vestibule and ventured to step across the threshold. His peripheral vision was sharp, and finely honed; it picked up movement to his right. A blow that was no doubt aimed at his torso instead hit his right forearm and his pistol flew into the darkness in the direction of the staircase. Reflexes kicked in. As the anonymous assailant was upon him, he clouted the man in the side of the head with his physician's bag and sent him careening into the wall with enough force to stun him. Before that attacker had hit the floor, a second one leapt out of the shadows to the left of the front door and grabbed Winter from behind, pinning his arms to his sides.

Winter tipped violently forward from the hips, flipping the would be assassin over into the center of the vestibule. Their struggle was loud but not terribly long. It ended when Winter picked up a Queen Anne side table from the wall adjacent to the drawing room door and swung it at his adversary's torso. The blow caused the man to double over with a grunt; Winter dropped the table, grabbed his attacker's head in both hands and snapped his neck.

As the second assassin lay dying, the first was regaining his feet. Winter saw him from the corner of his eye as he moved toward the stairs in search of his pistol. He had only enough time to face the Legion lackey before the man had drawn a gun and aimed it at his heart. There was no time to dodge; he was too far away to attack. He saw the man's teeth flash white in the darkness of the vestibule, caught the twitch of his trigger finger a mere instant before the gunman was engulfed in a bright blue electrical charge. He dropped straight to the floor like a marionette with severed strings.

Standing behind him in the front doorway was Nikola Tesla, holding his little energy pen. He looked up at Winter and smiled broadly.

"Never leave home without it!" he said cheerfully.

"I told you to stay outside," growled Winter.

"Sorry, but I thought all that noise in here was my signal to engage. If I hadn't I suspect you might be shot." He paused to look around at the bodies. "I must say, Dr. Atkinson, you have a decidedly rough bedside manner. I trust you are less assertive with your patients."

Smiling grimly, Winter reached down, snatched the fallen assassin's pistol from the floor and handed it to Tesla.

"Here, take this. It's a lot better than that French tickler you're carrying."

Tesla looked affronted. "It did the job, did it not? And I daresay it's a fine weapon, considering what I had on hand to build it." He took the more powerful pistol anyway, though grudgingly. "What will you do for a weapon, Doctor?"

Winter glanced toward the staircase and was pleased to see a glint of steel on the second step. He crossed to the staircase, picked up the gun, and held it up for Tesla to see.

"Now," he said, "keep your eyes open and get behind me. And if I tell you stay, *please* stay."

"Yes, Doctor. As you wish."

Winter led the way into the main drawing room, which was on the ground floor to the right of the stairs. The room was little lighter than the vestibule, despite the fact that moonlight filtered through the curtains through two tall windows to the right of the door. Winter had gotten nearly to the center of the room when the lights flicked on, all but blinding him. He spun, bringing his weapon to bear.

Tesla stood blinking at him from the light switch next to the door.

"What are you doing?" Winter demanded.

Tesla blinked again, then pointed over Winter's shoulder and said, "Well, now you can see *him* better."

"See . . . ?" He swung back toward the center of the room to behold a tall, spare man in a long black coat rise from behind a desk set along the far wall. His skin was ashen and mottled as if he had survived a fire. Light flashed on coin-sized metal patches at his temples.

"Who are you?" Winter asked, bracing himself for another attack.

The tall man smiled one of the most unsettling smiles Winter had seen in his long experience. "Someone what's spit in the face of God."

It was the smile that Winter remembered. He'd seen this man before—though his coloring had been far more normal, then. He'd been with the skyraider captain at the Resistance ambush in the train graveyard. His commander had called him 'Jack.'

Spit in the face of God? Winter shivered as a creeping comprehension of the skyraider's meaning began to dawn.

Tesla stepped forward, then, and did the most damnable thing; he drew his folio from the inner pocket of his coat and held it aloft.

"Are you looking for this, you ramshackle creation? Here, fetch!"

He lobbed the folio at the intruder, sailing it over Winter's head. But before Jack could snatch it, Tesla shot it with his little energy weapon. It was haloed in the frenetic blue light for no more than two seconds before it went up in a flash of flame. Ashes from the incinerated pages fell like dirty snow, covering the desk and its occupant in white and gray dapples.

Jack roared in protest, as did Winter.

"Tesla! My God, what are you *doing*?"

As if he'd suddenly decided he was invincible, the scientist pointed to his own head and said, "Don't worry. There's a copy, isn't there? Plus, every last equation is lodged between these ears."

Their adversary took this as his cue to attack. He flipped the heavy mahogany desk over as if it weighed no more than the unfortunate Queen Anne table in the vestibule, and leapt over it straight at Tesla. Winter was just swift enough to grab Jack by the shoulders and use his momentum to ram him headfirst into the wall. Then he swiftly aimed his gun and fired before the skyraider could right himself . . . or at least he tried to fire. Apparently its collision with the stairs had damaged the pistol's trigger.

Jack, still smiling, began to move toward him.

Fine, then.

Winter threw himself at Jack, swinging at his head with the butt of the pistol. The man didn't even attempt to dodge the blow. He took it full in the cheek, his smile never faltering. Winter struck him again and again with fists and the gun butt. He might as well have been using a pillow, so little effect did the blows have on the other man.

Finally, as if tiring of a toy, Jack grasped Winter by the lapels of his coat and bore him to the wall, knocking his head painfully against the plaster before wrapping his long fingers around Winter's neck. He squeezed.

"Tesla!" Winter rasped.

Tesla fired, first with the pistol, then with the energy pen. Oddly, it was the second shot that got a reaction from Jack. He jerked, lifted Winter into the air and tossed him aside as if he were a doll. Then he turned and lunged toward Tesla. Before the scientist could get off another shot, Jack knocked his weapons away and slugged him in the side of the head with enough force to knock him unconscious.

Tesla swayed for a moment, then collapsed over Jack's shoulder. The undead assassin—for surely he must be one of the Legion's reanimates—leapt through one of the large windows with his insensate captive dangling limply across his back like a sack of potatoes, sending shattered glass everywhere.

Winter, dizzy and disoriented, could only watch him go. It took him several moments to gather his strength and rise from the floor. He staggered to the bookcase behind the desk and flipped down a row of false books that sat at shoulder level, revealing a communication transceiver. He flipped the device on and spoke into the diaphragm.

"Artemus, are you there? Are you there, man?"

For several seconds, there was only the crackle of static. Then Artemus's voice came through.

"Yes, yes, I'm here. Sorry. I suppose you must be calling from the safe house. Is Tesla ready to travel?"

"The safe house has been compromised. Our men are dead, and the Legion has Tesla."

There was a sharp silence, during which Winter could hear other voices, muffled by their distance from the comms panel.

"My God, laddie," said Artemus at last. "Any idea where they have taken him?"

That, at least, was not a complete botch. "I placed a T-one homer on his coat. You should be able to track it. The key code is one-seven-six-six-one."

"Yes, I have it. What now?"

Winter considered that. Given what he suspected they were dealing with . . . .

"I think we may have underestimated our Mr. Cross. We may need to enlist the aid of some more powerful allies."

"Buckingham?" guessed Artemus.

"Buckingham. That is, if he's still alive. I haven't seen him since my funeral."

Thirteen - Barbarian

REGENT'S PALACE - ROTHERWOOD

VIKTOR VON BRANT WAS LOOKING FORWARD TO SUPPER. IF THERE was one thing he appreciated about Benton Cross it was that he surrounded himself with the finest in creature comforts. This included the chef he had brought with him to Rotherwood, along with the kitchen staff that supported him. Tonight, Viktor had been told, their table would be graced with roast pheasant and an American turkey.

He patted his cravat and smiled in anticipation. He'd never had wild turkey. He began to hum as he closed the ornately carved door to his rooms and turned to make his way to the stairs. The carpet beneath his feet was a plush, heavily figured runner of reds and golds that he understood had been hand-woven by beautiful Persian women in Tehran. He could almost imagine them, weaving away, dressed in silks and satins, their dark *houri* eyes gazing soulfully above the veils he had heard they wore.

He had just stepped into a cross-corridor when someone laced a muscular arm around his neck, stifled his surprised grunt with an equally strong hand, and dragged him into a deep window alcove. A shimmer of metallic music told him his assailant was Mordecai Judd. The voice in his ear confirmed it.

"I'd suggest you keep quiet, Doctor, unless you wish to perform an emergency surgery this evening. On yourself."

Viktor looked down to see that Judd held a long and very sharp blade against the quilted silk of his finest weskit. He nodded emphatically. Judd lifted the hand from his mouth, turned him about, and pressed him against the wall beside the window. The knife still hovered very near his heart.

"What do you want from me, Captain?" the scientist asked, trying not to feel his heart haring away in this chest, trying not to pant or otherwise betray his abject fear.

Judd leaned out of the alcove and glanced around the corner into the corridor before saying, "Well, first of all, I want you to keep your voice down. Second, I need a few answers."

"Very well. If I can."

"I want to ask you about these so-called Ether units you were working on with Tesla. When you described their effects, you used the words 'eternal life.'"

"*Ja*. We were very close. I had a strong feeling that Tesla actually had the problem of decay solved, but was just playing with us. Stalling. I now realize he was buying time for his escape."

"You say you were close. How close?"

Viktor shrugged—difficult with his shoulders rammed up against the wall. "If I could have just gotten the last two parts of the equation, I know I could produce a working self-recharging unit, immediately. Without it, it would take a minimum of six months."

"Six months?" repeated Judd. "Why so long?"

"This is *terra incognita,* Captain. Unknown territory. Untested. Untried. No man has traveled this path, *mein freunde.* Only God has done it."

"This is not religion, Doctor, this is science."

That raised Viktor's eyebrows. How surprising—to get philosophy from such a savage as this pirate lord. No, a pirate's parrot, more like. Perhaps he'd heard Cross discuss such things. It was doubtful he even understood the word *science.*

Von Brant shook his head. "If only your mind could match the skills of your mouth, captain."

Judd pressed the dagger against a button on Von Brant's vest, making him cringe and wish he could melt through the wall.

"I saved your hide once, little as you recall it. I rescued you from that rat's nest of a prison, but don't think for a second that I wouldn't kill you if you were to lie to me."

Prison? Von Brant stared, transfixed, at the man who held him pinned to the wall. Memory flooded his mind. Yes, take away the long hair, add a beard . . . .

"*Mein Gott!* Yes, that's how I know you! It *is* you! I had no name for you, then."

"Ah, but I had a name for you. You *owe* me, Dr. von Brant, and in repayment for your debt, you will inform me of your progress with your Ether experiments . . . every step of the way."

Viktor's relief made sweat break out on his brow. What matter to him if the Red Tong captain knew the course of his experiments? What could such a barbarian do with the information, after all?

"Of course, Captain Judd."

"And tell no one about our little chat this evening. Understand?"

"Certainly. But I assure you, such drama was unwarranted. You might have simply *asked*."

"Hm. You say that, but I am not inclined to be trusting. I want to be certain we have a deal—a covenant, if you will. Do we have a deal?"

Viktor met Judd's eyes solemnly and nodded, offering Judd his hand. "*Ja.*"

"Done, then. Did I mention that I don't shake hands?" Judd favored him with a brilliant smile and stepped back, flicking his knife away into concealment. "Well, I'm famished. I'll see you at supper, Viktor."

Mordecai Judd was gone so swiftly, Viktor was tempted to believe he had hallucinated the entire episode. He was certain of one thing; he no longer cared about the wild American turkey.

Fourteen - Buckingham

LONDON

WINTER OPENED THE DOOR OF THE ANTIQUE SHOP TO THE ringing of the tiny bell suspended above it. It was a cheerful sound that brought the unwelcome memory of a toy shop near Covent Garden that had just such a bell. He imagined he could feel the heat of the toy store's overactive furnace on his cheeks—a delight after the cold of a wintry day—see the barrage of bright colors from every display, inhale the scent of pine boughs and the bubbling apple cider the shopkeep served his guests during the holiday season. His recall of Emily's smiles and Jon's exclamations of amazement at the clever mechanical toys the shop specialized in was crystalline and painful.

Winter shook himself free of the unwanted distraction and struggled to see the place in which he now stood. The shop, though small, was brimming with the treasures of past centuries—paintings, vases, candelabras, delicate pieces of furniture. In stark contrast to the toy shop his memory had conjured, the decor of Rose's Antiques was muted. The walls were a soft dove grey above wainscoting the color of aged linen. A fire burned comfortingly in the small gas hearth on the right hand wall, and light fell softly from a chandelier hung with crystals that scattered rainbows about the room. Along the rear wall of the shop was a counter from behind which a petite young woman smiled at him. Next to the counter was an ornate dressing screen with an Asian motif, each silk panel framed by exotic wood.

"Good day, sir," the shop girl greeted him. "My name is Annabel. May I assist you?"

"Good day, miss. I certainly hope you might. I am looking for something quite rare; vanishingly hard to find."

"I should say you have come to the right place, then. We specialize in rare items. If it is not in our present inventory, the owner is more than happy to attempt tracking the item down. Can you tell me more about what you're seeking?"

Winter took the next step in the clandestine dance. "The item has a connection to British royalty and is above fifty years old. Oh, and it comes with a bit of ornamentation similar to this." He displayed his codex ring.

If Annabel was surprised, it did not show. A cool one, this young lady. She inspected the ring carefully, then said, "Mmmm, yes. Quite unusual. Though not unique. Actually, I have seen at least one other just like it. Why don't you step over to my counter, and I will see if I can help locate that piece for you."

Nodding, Winter crossed the room to stand before the clerk's counter. She smiled again, then pulled out a drawer, the contents of which he couldn't see from his vantage point. He heard a muted *click*, and watched her face as she regarded whatever was in the drawer. A moment later, she looked up at him again and smiled.

"It looks as if I may have found what you are looking for. If you'll just step behind that screen and go through the door, there, I believe you'll find what you seek."

Winter took a step behind the screen and found that it concealed a single door with a crystal doorknob. He turned slightly toward Annabel and inclined his head, touching the brim of his hat. From this point of view, he could see what she'd been looking at beneath her counter. A panel was even now sliding into place over the screens of several small tele-monitors, one of which showed the spot on which he'd been standing a moment before. He smiled tightly.

"Thank you for your assistance, miss."

Winter opened the door to find himself inside a small utility closet filled with brooms and other assorted cleaning utensils. There was an overhead light with a pull chain dangling from it. He reached up and tugged the chain, turning the light on, then closed the door behind him. He knew what this was. Knew what to look for. He found it on the back wall of the closet in what would appear to the untrained eye as a small knothole. He dialed in a code on his ring and inserted the crown into the knothole.

There was a *snick* of sound and the rear wall of the closet slid open, revealing a stately, well-appointed, windowless room. It had an orderly, military feel; what ornamentation decorated the walls was historical in nature—photos and paintings of soldiers, antique weaponry, a helmet or two. Over a fireplace that dominated the far wall, hung a saber and an officer's dress shako or helmet.

Winter stepped across the threshold onto a thick Persian carpet. The door slid shut behind him with an emphatic *click*. He looked up to the far left side of the room where a large desk of dark wood held a commanding view of the space. A man was seated behind the desk, engrossed in writing. His skin was the color of mahogany, his hair was tightly curled and glossy black except for a dusting of silver at the temples, his bare forearms bore witness to his physical fitness.

Florian Buckingham, Winter thought, had aged exceptionally well. "Brigadier," he greeted him.

Buckingham did not so much as glance up from his writing. "Well, there must be something truly Earth-shattering going on for you to come out of hiding, Brenden. You look like hell, by the way."

"I'm in disguise," Winter said wryly, glancing around the room. "But I thank you, sir. It's wonderful to see you too. So, the former head of the SIS now lives the life of a monk in secret seclusion?"

"How I decide to live my life is none of your concern, Lieutenant Commander." Buckingham at last set down his pen and looked up at his guest, steepling his fingers before him. "So, why are you here?"

Winter crossed the room to stand before Buckingham's desk. "The Resistance intercepted a Serbian scientist—Professor Nikola Tesla—after he made his escape from one of the Legion's facilities. It seems his research attracted the attention of Benton Cross, who abducted him and forced him to work on a top secret experiment."

Buckingham shrugged. "Good work, then. Cross has coopted many of our scientific minds to further his dystopian plans. I fail to see why this should bring you to me."

Winter took a step farther, his gaze on his ex-commander's face, willing him to feel the urgency of the situation. "This is different, Florian. What they are working on now is so ghastly, it would surely put an end to the Resistance and crush what remains of the free world we once knew. Perhaps forever."

Buckingham's eyebrows rose. "Sounds dire. But if you have Tesla, simply keep him out of harm's way. End of story."

Winter looked down at the desktop, fighting his own sense of guilt. "The Legion has gotten Tesla back again."

Buckingham rocked back in his chair. "Oh, jolly good. So, they've managed to steal him back from you, have they? What a right daft blunder! This would have never happened on my watch." He made a sarcastic *tsk*, then leaned forward and picked up his pen once more.

Winter failed to contain the flush of rage that overwhelmed him. "*Your* watch? You self-righteous bastard! The SIS was infiltrated on your watch. Good agents were killed on your watch. The Queen was assassinated on your watch!"

Finally, Buckingham showed some emotion beyond smug arrogance. He shot out of his chair, slamming his hands down on the top of his desk and scattering his papers. His pen clattered to the floor.

"Stand down, Lieutenant Commander!" he roared.

Winter set his own fists on the desktop and met Buckingham almost nose to nose across the desk.

"I am no longer your damned lieutenant commander! And you, sir, are not the man I was hoping to find here."

"And who is this man you were hoping to find, hm? A hard-nosed commander? A strategist? A tactician? A warrior? Well, I am none of those things now. Those days are behind me." He straightened, making a gesture as if to dismiss his anger. "Don't you think I live every day with the horror of those last months of the Service? Watching our elite force be infiltrated by spies and informants? Watching my soldiers, my officers, my *friends* fall at the hands of these Legion bastards? Then, to hear that the Queen had—" He sucked in a breath, shaking his head. "I watched as our England burned and crumbled from the inside out."

"But you were also the man who led our fight for three years," Winter countered earnestly. "You kept Cross and his bloodthirsty regime out of our lands, out of our cities, while other nations toppled all around us. You kept those bloody bastards at bay and showed them that this small but mighty island and her people would fight to their last breath rather than live as slaves under a dictatorship."

"Yes, but Cross saw the toll we were taking on his men, his operations, his grand plans." Buckingham looked down at the top of his desk for a moment, then shook his head and said, "Cross had one of his agents contact me. He offered me two-hundred-fifty thousand pounds Sterling if I would be his eyes and ears. I was to feed him information concerning the Queen's movements and whereabouts."

Winter straightened and took a step back from the desk. Was his old commander about to tell him he had been turned?

"Yes, I see the question in your eyes, Brenden. As much as it infuriates me to see it, I cannot fault it. But know that I told Cross's agent to go to hell and take his master with him. Unfortunately, there are always men willing to sell their souls to the devil. They may not be the ones you would suspect of such acts. The hardest enemies to defeat are the ones you do not suspect and cannot see."

"Well, I guarantee you will be able to see this enemy. Cross is amassing a new kind of army."

Buckingham's brow furrowed. "What kind of army—automatons? Surely the technology—"

"No. Not automatons. An army of the living dead."

Winter said the words without emphasis or drama. Buckingham laughed, nonetheless.

"What? You're joking, surely."

"I wish I were. No. This will be an army the likes of which the world has never seen. I have fought one of these things. Looking into its eyes was like gazing into the eyes of Death personified. There was no stopping it. You couldn't simply shoot it, short-circuit it, or confuse its programming. If Cross is able to create more of these things, then there's no telling how fast he can take control of the remaining free countries. And the key to it all is Nikola Tesla."

Buckingham lowered himself back into his chair, his eyes narrowed. "This was the nature of the experiments Cross was forcing Tesla to participate in? This . . . necromancy?"

Winter nodded. "Yes, but this is science, not magic. The procedure makes use of a sort of battery to reanimate the recently dead. At present, the reanimated do not last long. Mere months. But Cross's scientist is working on that problem, and if he solves it . . . ."

Buckingham's face was a blank as he considered this. His eyes flicked up to Winter's face. "So, what do you propose I do?"

Winter stepped forward again. "I propose you lead our men. Yes, Archangel can rally freedom fighters," he added, seeing the withdrawal in the brigadier's eyes, "throw fear into our enemies, and even damage their forces. But he cannot do it alone. He needs a military leader—a tactician, as you say—who can create a coherent battle plan."

"I hear Henry Ramsay—"

"Sir Henry Ramsay is dead."

The words caused a visible change in Buckingham's posture and expression. Shock and sorrow flickered in his gaze.

"God rest his soul," he murmured.

Winter took a step back toward the desk, renewing his verbal assault on Buckingham's will. "There is no man better than you to organize and lead a focused charge directly into the heart of the Legion. No one, Florian."

The brigadier shook his head. "My fighting days are long over. Why not contact one of the Paladins? They're out there. They have not all been killed. I might be able to put you in touch—"

"The Paladins were *your* elite fighting force. They will follow no one but you in this sort of engagement, and you know it."

Buckingham closed his eyes and rubbed at them with both hands. Winter watched him, certain he had finally reached him. But when his old commander opened his eyes again, there was a stone wall behind them.

"As I said, old man, I've hung up my blade for life. I hunt antiquities now, not Legion operatives. I am truly sorry, but I cannot help you." He punctuated the statement by leaning over and retrieving his pen from the floor.

Winter was struck dumb for a moment. When words finally came to mind, they were filled with both disappointment and a boiling anger. Anger wanted him to demand Florian Buckingham tell him how he had become such a coward. Wanted to rant at him, to blister him with hot, sharp words. But the anger faded as soon as it had bloomed, leaving him feeling spent and resigned. It was disappointment that spoke.

"Then, I suppose I must let you return to your world of solitude and writing. By all means, bury your head deep in the sand of your books, because the world you would live in no longer exists and you will find no comfort in it. I choose to live, and possibly die, for a larger cause with a band of men and women with whom I stand shoulder to shoulder. At least, I will have stood up for something even you once believed in, and for a nation that needs me in its time of peril."

He paused, watching as Buckingham bent once more to his writing, then conceded defeat. "May God be with you, my old friend," he said.

"And with you, Brenden. And with you."

Winter turned to leave, pausing only an instant at the door to glance back at the brigadier. He sat motionless, his dark eyes staring at the rear wall of his study. Winter followed his gaze to where his saber and shako hung above the hearth, metal fittings gleaming in the soft light from the fire. He opened his mouth to register one more plea, then shook his head and left Florian Buckingham to his solitude.

Back out on the street, Winter pulled his scarf up around his chin, bent his head into the chill wind and began to walk—where, he didn't care. He needed to think in straight lines, but right now his thoughts were shooting off in all directions. Should he wait a while then try again with Buckingham? Contact the Paladins? (Yes, there were still some about and he knew where they were.) Resign himself to attempting a role he knew he was not best suited for? He was used to working the field alone with a support team around him, not in marshalling and organizing troops and battle plans.

He had walked perhaps two miles when he finally became aware of his surroundings. He was in a graceful neighborhood of shops and businesses that he realized he recognized. In his seemingly random ramble, he had strayed toward familiar territory. Just up the street a ways was a park in which he, his wife, and son once took their evening walks and fed the fat, happy ducks. And just behind him was a bookstore they used to frequent.

He stopped dead in his tracks on the sidewalk, causing a couple of dowagers behind him to harrumph and give him annoyed glances as they stepped around him with an outraged rustling of taffeta. He should leave at once. He should turn and flee back to St. Pancras. He should. But that desire to flee was at war with an equal and opposite desire to continue on up this street, to turn the corner on the opposite side of the park, to set eyes on his home—or what had been his home and could be no longer.

The war went on for some minutes as people parted to pass him by, some giving him curious looks as he stared up toward the park.

"I say. Sir? ... Sir?"

He blinked and turned his head to see a middle-aged gentleman regarding him with concern.

"Are you lost, sir?"

"Lost?" God, yes, he was lost. He shook his head. "No, just trying to decide if I've time to browse the bookstore yonder before I . . . before I go home."

The man smiled. "Ah, yes! I've just come from there myself." He raised a brown paper parcel that looked as if it contained at least two volumes. "They're open for an hour yet. I'm sure you've time for a good browse."

Winter doffed his hat. "I thank you, sir. And good afternoon to you."

"To you too, sir." The man returned the gesture, then strode off down the street whistling.

Well, that decided it. He didn't know the kind stranger, but he might have. His Atkinson disguise was proof to most people, but would it be to someone who had known him well? Florian had seen through it, but then he'd seen Winter in disguise countless times and there were damn few people alive who had access to an SIS codex ring.

He turned on his heel and headed back the way he had come, slowing as he reached the bookshop. On the chance that his guide might see him, he decided to go into the shop. Perhaps he might even purchase something if the owner, who knew the entire Winter clan quite well, wasn't in.

He paused with his hand on the door latch to peer into the shop. Seeing a clerk he didn't recognize at the till, he started to pull the door open, then froze. In a mullioned pane in the upper half of the door, his wife and son were framed as if in an animated portrait. They were, in fact, making their way straight to the entrance, their heads bent over a volume they must have just purchased.

Winter stood transfixed at the sight of his family. Emily with her dark curls caught up beneath a black silk bonnet, Jonathan with his fair hair gleaming in the light of the shop. She was so beautiful, his Emily, even in mourning. And Jon, at twelve, was already beginning to look less a boy and more a young man. They were smiling, a sight that both warmed and wounded.

They had almost reached the door, and Emily was tucking the book into her shopping satchel, when Winter broke the spell they had cast. He started to turn, to flee, but an elderly woman had bustled up behind him, obviously intent on entering the bookstore.

He did the only thing that made sense and that would not draw undue attention to him. He opened the door for the old woman and doffed his hat, barely daring to look up from beneath the brim as Emily and Jon exchanged greetings with the matron and stepped out onto the sidewalk.

"Thank you, sir," said Emily and the sound of her voice nearly brought him to his knees.

"Ma'am," he said in return, his voice hoarse, disguised by raw emotion. He did not dare meet her gaze, as desperately as he wanted to.

"Yes, thank you," said Jon politely. His voice had deepened noticeably since his father had last heard him speak.

Winter nodded and returned his hat to his head as they swept past him and continued on toward the park and their house. Heart laboring, legs suddenly weak, he turned to watch them as they moved away from him, feeling the connection between them running out like a kite string.

He watched them until they reached the corner on the far side of the park. Watched them, with hungry eyes, until they turned the corner and the kite string snapped.

FIFTEEN - BATTLE PLAN

LONDON - ST. PANCRAS

WINTER ENTERED THE LAB BENEATH ST. PANCRAS CEMETERY to find his team standing around the circular table in the center of the room. The table was littered with the papers, notebooks, and maps the team was studying. The sight brought him back to the present—to the *real*—in a way the brisk walk back to his safe haven had not. *This* was his present reality; Emily and Jonathan were part of a past he could never retrieve.

Artemus had swung about to greet him. "Ah, there you are. How did you fare with Sir Buckingham?"

"I . . . ah . . . I'm afraid we will go it alone with this mission. The brigadier refuses to be involved."

Artemus frowned, pulled his glasses down onto his nose, and peered at Winter with obvious concern. He opened his mouth to speak, but Kenzie cut across him.

"I can't understand that," the young Scotsman said. "We were certain he would want to take up the Cause with us."

"Nonetheless," said Winter, stepping down into the lab, "we must move forward. Artemus, what have we got?"

He moved to stand next to McDowell at the table. The others—Kenzie, Ginny, and Bobby—acknowledged him with solemn expressions.

The professor tapped the topmost diagram with the tip of his finger. "We tracked Tesla to one of Cross's munitions facilities in Enfield. This is the basic layout. It was a cotton mill before Cross turned it into one of the Legion's main weapons factories. It has a rather simple design, as you can see."

Winter peered at the diagram. It was essentially a tactical map overlaid on an aerial photograph of a building that, from the top, looked like a squat letter H.

"What type of security does the place have?"

Artemus pulled another large sheet of paper toward him—a wider angle view of the same building, showing its setting in a densely wooded area. A single, narrow road led to and from the factory, winding through the forested hills.

"He has three aerial balloons in place." He tapped the three objects on the map. One covered the front of the building, one covered the rear, and hovered directly over the central crossbar. "Each is manned by one heavily armed guard, and they are equipped with standard searchlights for night watch. They'll have to be dispatched first, of course. And as quietly as possible."

"Which is why," said Ginny, holding up a small dart, "Bobby and I have manufactured a set of these. Ballistic syringes. They can be armed with immobilon or cyanide or a combination of the two. Immobilon will block the target's voluntary motor control, so no hue and cry. Without the cyanide its effects would last for roughly half an hour. With the cyanide, obviously—"

"The target dies almost instantly," said Bobby Mortimer. He turned and moved to Ginny's worktable, where he grabbed a sleek pistol and another of the darts. "These can be fired from our standard high-powered air pistols, which means delivery is virtually silent and with no muzzle flash. Accurate range is up to one hundred and fifty meters."

Kenzie gave Ginny a sideways glance. "Ah, just like a woman. Silent and lethal."

She responded with a roll of her green eyes and an annoyed twist of her mouth. She held up her dart as if to throw it at him. "Care to demonstrate for us, Mr. Graham? This one contains immobilon. It would make it impossible for you to utter a word for half an hour. I might hope for longer, but I'll take what I can get."

He met her disdain with a satisfied grin. "Why, I love ya' too, Miss Gelsen, honey."

Artemus cleared his throat. "Lady and gentlemen, if I may." He returned his focus to the map. "As for the perimeter of the Enfield facility, it's patrolled by power-suits. Usually only two, since the main access leading in and out of the facility is limited to one road. They are placed directly opposite each other—" He tapped the two tiny figures.

Power-suits. That wasn't good news. Winter had hoped for automatons. By virtue of having to be laboriously programmed, they were not particularly good at responding to the unexpected. Human guards in power-suits, however, had the advantages of an automaton's ablative armor, with the added advantage of being able to think independently and tactically.

"It looks," said Winter, noting the position of the two power-suits on the map, "as if they never make visual contact."

"Aye. We must assume they communicate in some way, though."

"Then we shall have to take them out before they can communicate." Winter pointed at a spot on the map, indicating the thickly forested area that cupped the rear of the building. "What about this woods, here? Can we use it for cover?"

Artemus nodded. "That would be our best option, though we'll need to stay out of the visual range of the power-suits."

Winter nodded, considering this, then turned to Bobby Mortimer. "How did you make out with the smoke bombs I asked for, Bobby?"

Bobby moved to the table opposite Ginny's chemistry layout, picked up a handful of small, intricate metal spheres the size of large walnuts, and held them out for Winter to see.

"They're ready to go, sir. Pressing this small button here . . ." He demonstrated on one of the spheres. ". . . activates a five second timer. Each one of these buggers will produce a large enough and impenetrable enough smoke screen to mask any type of maneuver. It would hide a steam carriage, up to a dozen men, whatever we need."

Well, that was good news. Not even a man in a power-suit could see through impenetrable smoke. He was beginning to believe this could be done. He *had* to believe it could be done.

"Excellent, Bobby. Artemus, what can we expect to find once inside the facility?"

"The plant is three stories tall. The rear courtyard seems to be where the distribution of their wares takes place. Given the comings and goings of the lorries and what Dr. Tesla was able to tell us, it's clear the main purpose of this plant was the assembly of both power-suits and beamer weapons. But a sizable amount of munitions are housed there, too. We know that Cross has also dedicated at least one lab for these new experiments. Given he means to raise an army, we can assume he's got some sort of plan in place for mass production. The only logical place for such a wretched assembly line—given its need for massive amounts of electrical power—would be in this general vicinity; close to the plant's main power source."

He drew a circle around a juncture between the west wing and central section of the building, where the left-hand vertical of the H met the cross bar. Winter could see from the protrusions on the rooftop and the distinctly different materials that clad the surfaces there that something was being allotted extra protection and that the something generated and/or used much electricity.

"We'll need to concentrate on that area, then," Winter said, "since it's most likely where Tesla will be. I will take care of the perimeter power-suits. However, we will need a diversion to pull as much security away from that wooded area as we can."

Kenzie spoke up. "Leave that to me, sir. After we disable those balloons, me and a few of my boys can plant a number of timed charges to go off in the woods at the front of the building to draw out their security forces where our men can engage them. That should buy us enough time to get in, kibosh the power plant, destroy the lab and weapons depot, and find the Professor."

He placed another diagram and a couple of elevation sketches atop the pile. These were illustrations Kenzie had drawn from Tesla's description of the parts of the plant he had seen. They were highly detailed and displayed quite a bit of natural talent and skill. His sketch of the lab showed where Tesla remembered machines and devices to have stood and even hinted at the materials in use—brick, wood, metal.

Where that skill for drawing came from, even Kenzie could not recall. He'd come under Artemus's wing after emigrating to London from Edinburgh and sustaining an almost lethal blow to the head that had deprived him of some, though not all, of his memory. Whatever he'd lost, he had not been deprived of several uncanny abilities that made him invaluable to Archangel's intimate crew: he possessed both a charming way of being helpful to persons both high and low, keen powers of observation, and eidetic visual recall. If MacKenzie Graham once saw a person, place, or thing, he could reproduce it with pencil on paper. It was an odd talent to have, considering he could barely remember a thing about his own life in Edinburgh.

"If the lab is here," —Kenzie marked the spot on the map with a fingertip— "then it's likely beneath this lead cladding. Since the prof didn't see any sign of a power plant in the part of the place he traveled, I reckon it must be right about here." He moved his finger to the very center of the intersection between the leftmost wings of the building.

Winter nodded, thoughtfully. "Good. Yes. If we take that down, anything they've got that's drawing power goes down with it." He flicked a glance at Ginny Gelsen. "Will you be all right leading the third raiding party?"

The young woman straightened to her full height and tilted her head up to look him squarely in the eye. "I'll be fine, sir. Why wouldn't I be?"

Winter stifled a smile. "No reason at all. Forgive me for even asking."

Bobby let out a frustrated chuff of breath. "I wish this leg wasn't slowing me down. I'd love to use some of these babies on those slugs myself." He caressed his little smoke bombs as if they were treasured pets.

"You know, Ginny," said Kenzie, leaning his elbows on the table and gazing up into her eyes, "you could always come with me and let one of Archangel's commandos lead the third team."

She met the Scotsman's gaze with the iciest look Winter thought he'd ever seen on her pretty face. "And why would I do that? I'm perfectly capable of leading a strike team, thank you, MacKenzie Graham."

"Kenzie," said Winter, "stop needling Ginny. As it happens, she's right. She's perfectly capable of leading a strike team."

"I only meant," said Kenzie, "that being as how I'm not much of a fighter, I could surely use a wily ninja at my back."

Ginny pulled a face. "Flattery now, is it?"

"Let's stay on point," said Winter. "Once Tesla is safe, we must ensure that this place ceases operations. We need to plant sufficient timed charges at both the munitions storage area—once we locate it—and the power generators to destroy them entirely. Enough to level this place and set the Legion back for quite a while. If those charges aren't sufficient, then we'll have to blow the lab separately. This means accurate reconnaissance is crucial."

He looked around at the group. "Is there anything else?"

They all shook their heads.

"Fine, then. Kenzie, Ginny, tell your men to be ready to leave by zero-three-hundred hours. Attack time will be at zero-five-hundred precisely."

Kenzie, suddenly solemn as a judge, gave him an emphatic nod. "We'll be ready, sir."

He hoped that was so. "God be with you all."

The group dispersed to their individual tasks while Winter moved to the alcove at the far end of the lab's upper gallery. He flipped a toggle on the wall beside the alcove, illuminating what lay within—the Mark II body armor that turned him from a dead man's ghost into Archangel.

He shrugged out of his greatcoat to begin the metamorphosis.

"Ginny, may I have a word?"

Ginny turned from her study of a chemical reaction to find Kenzie Graham (the maddening creature) standing behind her.

"And what word would you like, Mr. Graham?" she asked tartly. "I have a mouthful."

"Aye," he said looking down at the floor, "and I can't say I don't deserve every one of them."

She'd opened her mouth to offer a sassy retort, when it registered how uncharacteristically solemn he was. Arms crossed over his chest, head tilted to one side, he showed nothing of his usual cockiness. She studied him for a moment through narrowed eyes, then swivelled her lab chair to face him.

"Go on, then."

"Ginny . . . ." He cleared his throat. "The thing is, Ginny . . . ."

"Yes, that's my name. No need to remind me."

He sucked in a breath, then swept his cap from his head. Chestnut hair tumbled into his eyes.

Lord love a duck. Ginny clamped her lips shut. Wonderful. Now he looked helpless and pathetic and ill at ease and . . . .

"I just wanted to apologize for . . . before. I *know* you're a bonny warrior in your own right. Bloody hell—I mean, *murder*—I meant what I said: you could fight circles 'round me."

"I suspect that's true," Ginny said, willing to be mollified.

Now he looked up, worrying his cap in his hands, and took a step toward her. "Oh, it *is!* And don't I know it! I want you to know that I know that you . . . you're an *amazement,* Ginny. And I've every respect for you as a fighter and a team leader and a scientist and a—and a woman. Why you're worth two of most men, you are."

The unexpected praise made her cheeks flame. "Well then, MacKenzie Graham, why did you say those things right out in front of everyone that suggested I *wasn't* . . . all that—" She made a flustered gesture. "—what you said."

"Honest?"

"Well, I should hope you'd be honest."

He moved to lean against the edge of her worktable, looking down at her with regret spilling out of his too-solemn blue-grey eyes.

"I want you to see me. I want you to notice me."

Ginny was stunned. "You want me to holler at you?"

"No! Of course not. I mean, I'd rather you not. But you see, you're smart—a prodigy, Artemus says—and you've got so much to offer the Resistance. And I've got so bloody little. All I've got—*all*—is being quick and stealthy and not fearful of much. Except I've come to realize I'm fearful of making you really hate me for being such a mouthy lout."

Ginny stunned became Ginny appalled. "But, I'd never—!"

He hurried on. "So, if I've caused you real grief, Ginny Gelson, I'm sorry. And I wish I could promise I'd never tease you anymore, but I can only promise I'll try. It's hard, because it's the only way I know to make you see me and talk to me."

She stared at him speechlessly for a time, not an idea in her head of what she should or could or wanted to say. And he, the unhelpful imp, just watched her flounder. After a moment, he straightened, put his cap back on his head, gave her a crooked smile, and walked away.

Sixteen - Dead Heroes

LONDON

Florian Buckingham dodged a steam carriage and two horsemen on his way across the street in front of Rose's Antiques. He carried a paper sack full of scones in one hand and his ebony walking stick in the other, the brass tip barely touching the cobbles. The bakery up the row had had Annabel's favorite scones today, so he had purchased a half dozen of them with a small packet of clotted cream and another of raspberry jam. They were so fresh that the bagged steamed in the chilly air.

He was thinking—or perhaps trying not to think about his conversation with Brenden Winter earlier. Winter obviously thought of his ex-commander as some sort of hero. Someone larger than life. Perhaps it was the knighthood that made it seem as if he was a rare specimen. Heroes, he would have told Winter, are not necessarily knights of the realm, but just ordinary people. They breathe; they bruise and bleed. And even if their own lives are impossibly knotted, they have the ability to untangle the lives of others.

He had lost that ability.

He cared not a bit if he bled or died, and his life now was relatively simple. He read, he wrote, he located and sold antiques and antiquities. Winter, himself, was a more likely hero. Florian Buckingham was a shade.

He set aside his dark musings, put a smile on his lips, and turned the door knob. It was locked. Annabel must have decided to close for tea time. He unlocked the door and stepped into the shop, to the familiar jingle of the bell over the door. The place was dark and quiet, the only light and sound came from the fireplace on the wall to his right.

Annabel had no doubt gone to his study to set up for tea. He found himself relishing the thought. She might be young and female, but she was smart, well-educated, and competent in ways that most women, even in this day and age in England, had little exposure to.

He relocked the shop door and made his way to the pass-through to his secret haven. The door was ajar. That was unusually careless of Annabel. True, she had locked the front door of the shop, but she had been well-trained to follow protocol instinctively.

He pushed the door open the rest of the way, immediately realizing that the secret panel was also open. A cold dread began to ooze its way up the brigadier's spine.

"Annabel!"

He dropped the bag of scones and hefted his walking stick. The press of a button and a tug at the ornate brass grip freed the blade concealed in the shaft. Now he had a sword in one hand and a solid cudgel in the other.

"Annabel!" he called again, then stepped quickly through into his study.

Here, too, the only light was from the hearth; it flickered on the half-concealed face of a hooded figure that sat behind his desk with its booted feet up on the mahogany top.

"I've been called many names in my life," said the anonymous man, in a broad northern accent, "but never Annabel."

"Who are you?" Buckingham growled.

The man lowered his hood, revealing a charred and sunken face.

Buckingham fought the natural desire to recoil from the sight and made himself take a step forward. "Maybe the question is *what* are you?"

The smile that question evoked made the flesh on Buckingham's back crawl.

"Let's just say I'm a messenger from Benton Cross. We know you've been approached by the Resistance. He suggests that you just go back into hiding and forget all about this Rezzie nonsense."

"That's ironic. You see, I'd already made up my mind to 'forget all about this Rezzie nonsense' before you intruded. Your boss apparently doesn't know me very well, or he would know that I—and no one else—decides what I will or will not do. Now get out of my office, before I run you through for trespassing."

The unnatural smile broadened into a grin. "I thought you'd say something like that. I admit, I was half hoping you would."

He snapped his fingers and two men appeared from the shadows at the corners of the room, flanking Buckingham. Both wielded electro-batons. He cursed himself for being caught unawares, but before he could distance himself from them, his body was covered in blue lightning. Every nerve in his body was set ablaze. He doubled over in pain, falling to his knees, his numbed fingers losing their grip on his weapons.

"Bind his wrists," the charred man said.

Buckingham fought to clear his head and regain control over his limbs, but his brain and body refused to submit to his mind's commands. His assailants were able to truss him up like a prize boar.

The charred man rose from behind the desk and sauntered to the center of the room, clearly gloating at how easily he had captured the great Sir Florian Buckingham.

"Mr. Cross must really like you. He only wants me to cripple you. Not like we done your old chum, Ramsay. I made that old dog howl for hours in pain, 'fore I killed him."

"Bastard," Buckingham hissed.

He fought his senses under control and pushed up from the floor. The charred man elbowed him in the side of the head, knocking him down again. Lying on his side, groggy, he could only wallow and glare up at his attackers.

"Well, boys, it looks like *this* old dog still has some bite left in 'im. Give him another jolt or two of the ole' stim rods."

Both men lowered their batons toward Buckingham's body; he steeled himself for the disruptive blast of pain. There was a sudden rush of movement from the pass-through closet and the man on his right grunted as the stim rod flipped out of his hand to tumble away into the dim recesses of the room.

The man turned toward his swift assailant only to take a sword stroke to his throat. Blood sprayed in bright droplets as the body fell to the carpet. Annabel crouched above it, a dagger-sharp Roman gladius in one hand. Buckingham recognized it as being from a display on the shop floor. The second man whirled on her, swinging wildly at her with his baton. She met the attack with the flat blade of her sword, knocked the baton aside and impaled her assailant with a straight-ahead thrust that skewered him just below his breast bone.

It took the girl a moment to disengage the blade from her victim's body, and in that time, the charred man scooped up Buckingham's sword cane and went on the attack. The girl freed her blade and danced out of the way of his hasty thrust. He was clearly neither fencer nor ninja. Annabel Spellman was both.

It took her two moves to disarm him, sending Buckingham's slender epee under his desk. As the charred man turned to chase after it, Annabel ran her gladius through his back. The man cried out, spinning about with enough force to tear the weapon from Annabel's hand. He staggered back toward her, hands wrapped around the blade that protruded from his chest.

Something was wrong with the picture, Buckingham thought, but his floundering mind could not make out what it was.

The charred man doubled over, still moving toward Annabel, who stepped cautiously aside. He'd drawn level with her when he suddenly straightened, grabbed her by the shoulders and pulled her into his body for a deadly kiss. The sword's sharpened tip plunged into her breast with a gout of blood and Buckingham, horrified, finally understood what was wrong with the charred man's wound. Unlike Annabel, he did not bleed.

"God, no!"

The words exploded from Buckingham's lips in a rush of grief and loathing. He was able to roll up to his knees, but could only watch in stunned impotence as Annabel went limp in her killer's arms. The charred man pushed her away and watched her fall, broken, to the carpet, soaking it with her life's blood.

Her blood was on his lips as he turned to look down at Buckingham.

"The kiss of death is bloody sweet," he said, chuckling at his gruesome pun.

He licked his mouth clean, never taking his dead eyes from the brigadier's face. His tongue, Buckingham realized with further horror, was grey.

The horrific creature stretched to reach behind his back as if to scratch an itch. He grasped the hilt of Annabel's sword and pulled it from his back, then tossed it on top of her body.

Buckingham marshaled his senses enough to spit out five words: "I'll kill you, you monster."

The charred man reached into the breast pocket of his long coat and pulled out a pistol, which he aimed at Buckingham's heart.

"Not today, I think, Brigadier."

He fired.

The impact thrust Buckingham backwards against the wall, where he lay, staring up at the inhuman assassin. The charred man pocketed the pistol, then came to bend over him, touching a hand to his forelock in satirical salute.

"Give my regards to the Queen, when you see her, Brigadier. And tell her Iron Rail Jack sent you."

He took a final look around at the carnage, grinned, and left the room, ducking slightly to get through the door into the pass-through.

Buckingham tracked the sound of his footsteps to the door and heard the cheerful tinkle of the shop bell, thanking God that Iron Rail Jack was no more observant than a stunned and possibly concussed man twice his age. If he had been observant, he would have noticed that his would-be victim bled no more than he had. He might have even noticed that beneath the torn vest that covered Florian Buckingham's chest, was a padded undergarment of woven metal.

Buckingham counted to five before he moved, sliding with painful slowness over to Annabel's lifeless body. One of her arms lay across her stomach, the SIS codex ring on the slender hand a shiny blur in the waning light of the fire. He lay his head on her shoulder and wept.

SEVENTEEN -
DEAD MEN'S GHOSTS

ENFIELD

DAPHNE STOOD ON THE UPPER LEVEL OF VIKTOR VON BRANT'S research lab, still as a statue, showing no more emotion than if she'd been made of stone herself. Her eyes were fixed on that damnable lab table which, once again, had a man—or what had once been a man—lying upon it. This specimen was as tall as Iron Rail Jack, but far bigger and more muscular.

Grouped around the table were von Brant and his worshipful acolytes—Benton Cross and Mordecai Judd. Daphne pretended disinterest in their experiments, though it was not disinterest that kept her from joining them on the laboratory floor. Even looking at the fresh corpse—a warehouse worker who had suffered an undisclosed but convenient accident—gave her chills. She heard a swish of air to her left and turned to see Iron Rail Jack, himself, escort Nikola Tesla into the lab and march him straight to the operating table.

The Serbian scientist was disheveled, his thick hair was awry, and he sported a black eye and a cut on his right cheek. She shook her head minutely. Cross had yet to learn that some people did not surrender to violence, but only went deeper into themselves or lied. She sensed that Tesla was one of these. She knew he'd given them precious little information on his processes, offering only dribs and drabs of information.

"Ah, *Herr Doktor*, you have come!" exclaimed von Brant as if Tesla had had any say in the matter. "We can now begin."

Daphne steeled herself against the lightnings and thunders that accompanied the German scientist's romp about the lab, toggling this, switching that, activating

God knew what. If she were a cat, she would have raised her hackles, laid her ears back, and hissed. As it was, she simply watched the proceedings with as bland a look on her face as she could affect.

It seemed to take the professor longer this time to get his strange collection of machines to dance; perhaps whatever information Jack had squeezed from the unwilling Tesla had added to his mysterious process. The added length clearly annoyed Cross, who stood watching with his jaw a-twitch. Daphne knew that look; it made her even more glad she was not on the floor with the others.

"How close are we, Doctor?" Cross said after several minutes had elapsed.

Von Brant was peering up at a set of gauges on one of his several control panels that seemed not to be performing the way he expected. He frowned, tapped a gauge and said, "What? Ah! We are almost there! Just a few more minutes!"

"Hurry up," Cross demanded. "We don't have the luxury of time."

He turned to a worktable adjacent to the operating table and picked up a small wooden box roughly the size and thickness of his hand. He slid back the wooden lid and smiled at the contents. From where she stood, Daphne could not make out what that was, but unless her eyes deceived her (and in here that wasn't impossible), it gave off a faint glow.

"Dr. Tesla," Cross said, "I must thank you for your cooperation, unwilling as it was. We will now see if your final equations and the new Ether implants will work." He paused to turn his smile on Iron Rail Jack. "I hope Jack did not make you suffer too badly for the information."

"My personal suffering in no way contributed to my cooperation, as you call it. I lost a few drops of blood. That is nothing compared to how you will make this world bleed. And for what?"

Cross scoffed. "You truly don't know?"

"Oh, power, surely. Wealth, most likely. A sense of superiority, I suspect."

"And are these insignificant to you, Professor Tesla?"

Tesla's mouth twitched. "'Six feet of earth must now suffice for whom the earth was not enough.'"

He spoke quietly, but Daphne heard him clearly over the increasing hum and crackle of electricity in the room. Fine hairs rose up on the back of her neck and her arms.

"What?" Cross demanded, scowling. "What did you say?"

"The dying words of Henry Plantagenet, an English king who was, I suspect, a wiser man than either of us."

Cross opened his lips to retort, then shut his mouth and turned to von Brant. "Aren't you ready yet?"

The older man turned from the console he'd been prodding and hastened back to the operating table. "Ah! Yes, yes, yes. We are ready."

"Then, by all means, proceed."

Von Brant picked up the metal helm with its conducting rods and slipped it into place over the cadaver's head. Daphne knew that two discs identical to the ones that Iron Rail Jack wore had already been implanted in the man's head. Well, perhaps not quite identical. She gathered that something they'd brewed up from Tesla's notes had been added to the mix. She had no idea—nor did she care—what difference that might make in what was about to happen to the unfortunate warehouse worker.

Having made certain the conducting rods in the helm were positioned over the Ether implants, von Brant signaled a trio of his lackeys to toggle the switches that would allow the buildup of electromagnetic energy to flow to the main control panel next to the table. The lackeys toggled, the turbines whined, Daphne cringed inwardly, and von Brant fitted his dark goggles over his eyes and moved to the main controls.

"Ladies and gentlemen, please guard your eyes!"

He waited a beat for everyone to respond to his warning, then threw the main switch. Electrical energy sizzled in the air, making every last hair on Daphne's body rise up of its own accord. Her skin crawled with the energy, as if tiny ants made of lightning crept over her. The urge to flee the room was almost more than she could bear.

But bear it she did. One did not dare show fear or weakness around Benton Cross. So she gritted her teeth, closed her eyes tightly and gripped the gallery rail.

From his tree-top vantage point, Archangel followed the movements of the two power-suits walking patrol around Cross's Enfield facility. They marched the perimeter of the grounds with ground-eating strides, opposite each other as the aerial images had shown, roughly 100 yards from the building. Eight feet tall, and large enough to accommodate a full grown man comfortably, they had thick ablative armor, electrically powered motors, and a stunning array of armaments. They were also equipped with running lights that illuminated the ground in front of them. One of them always had his eyes on the entire rear of the property.

Those were the disadvantages. The advantages were that there were only two of them and they were out of sight of each other during their circuits of the property, blocked by the building they guarded. That meant the Resistance fighters needed only to defeat one of them, for if one could be removed without a chance to raise the alarm, the other would have no way of knowing he was marching alone. They were also highly visible and made excellent targets.

He turned his attention to the three manned sentry balloons—one at the front, one over the core of the building, and one closest to him at the rear. There was but a single soldier in each gondola. Those would have to be taken out first, unobtrusively enough that the power-suits would know nothing of it.

Archangel switched his focus to the rear courtyard formed by the legs of the H-shaped building. Here, there were human guards posted around a broad loading dock on the right hand side of the central section of the building. A bevy of steam lorries were parked in the yard, awaiting their potential loads. Given the sheer number of those lorries, it was highly likely that a massive amount of armaments and ordnance was stored somewhere close to those loading docks.

Using the carefully calibrated lenses in his optics, Archangel homed in on the broad rear entrance. He'd no more than gotten the image in focus when the exterior lights that illuminated the rear of the building dimmed and flickered. Simultaneously, a series of bright flashes illuminated the clerestory windows just to the left of the warehouse area. For a moment, it looked as if blue lightning danced behind the grimy panes. Something was happening within.

"Gentlemen," Archangel murmured into the speaking diaphragm of his helm, "if you are in position, we must move now."

MacKenzie Graham was first to respond. "Vanguard One is set," he said. "There is one hell of a fireworks show going on in there, sir."

"I see it. Vanguard Two, are you set?"

The commander of the second strike team, an ex-policeman named LeStrade, answered from his position in the woods further toward the center of the rambling structure.

"Vanguard Two is set."

"Affirmative," said Archangel. "Gentlemen, take out those aerial sentries."

Following his own orders, Archangel pulled out a pistol armed with ballistic syringes and took aim at the balloon over the roof of the facility. He pulled the trigger, surprised at how quiet the report was. The gun made only a slight puffing sound as it deployed its dart. His aim was true; the syringe hit the balloon sentry in the neck. The man reached up to slap it away, but his hand never reached its goal. He sagged in the harness that held him safely upright.

Some yards to Archangel's left, one of LeStrade's commandos echoed the process, taking out the rear sentry. A glance up over the rooftop showed that Kenzie had also struck, causing the balloon guarding the front of the building to bob gently as the guard went limp in his safety harness.

A second later, Archangel heard the sharp crack of a blaster rifle, saw a tracer of energy shoot upward into the canopy of the third balloon, and winced as the energy bolt ignited its gases in a huge, incandescent explosion. Flaming remnants of the thing jetted toward the factory and the balloon that hung over its ridgepole. A second later, that balloon ignited as well, battering the roof and raining debris onto the building below.

"What just happened?" Archangel demanded.

"T'wasn't me!" said Kenzie. "I think his gun must've gone off when he collapsed."

"Damn it," Archangel swore. "We've lost the element of stealth. Change of plans gentlemen—move out now!"

Trying hard not to hear the sounds of electric chaos, Daphne almost missed the sharp thud of something hitting the roof far above her head. She did not miss the sound of shattering glass. That was loud enough to overcome the crackle of electrical energy. Her eyes darted to the clerestory windows on the opposite side of the room from where she stood. Fiery debris tumbled through the broken panes, colliding with the tangle of wires over the center of the lab and interrupting the arcing currents.

Sparks erupted where electricity met the flaming pieces of wood and metallic fabric that surely must have come from one of the sentry balloons. Worse, the misdirected currents began to arc to the floor of the lab, perilously close to the group gathered around the operating table.

Daphne crouched in the madly flickering light, making herself as small a target as possible, though none of the ersatz lightning had struck anywhere near her. As she gathered her wits, one of the streamers of energy struck a member of von Brant's team. The man screamed—a razor-edged cry of agony that ended when he simply vaporized, leaving a puff of ash to filter to the floor.

He'd been standing within two feet of Benton Cross.

Daphne moved reflexively—slipping beneath the gallery rail and making straight for the operating table, her only thought to get Cross safely out of the chamber. Everyone else could die; Cross must be saved.

Von Brant had flipped the power switch that fed the reanimation helm and was shouting orders at his staff. "Schalte es aus! Jetzt! Shut it down! Now!"

The remaining members of his staff moved to do just that, but before their actions could have an effect, the cadaver on the table jerked, then shot bolt upright with a blood-curdling scream, ripping his restraints from their mountings. Flailing, he threw himself from the table to stand, roaring, facing the group of stunned watchers. Cross and Judd back-pedaled, but another member of von Brant's team did not move quickly enough; the massive reanimate grabbed him and hauled him into a death grip. Daphne could hear his bones snapping even over the chaos in the room.

Another scientist appeared from behind a bank of machinery, wielding an energy rifle, but before he could fire, the creature killed him as well. Then, the ex-human being swung about, its dilated eyes fixing on Cross.

Daphne pulled out her own pistol and began to fire at the thing as she advanced into the room. Her blasts only caused it to stumble and hesitate before it righted itself and kept moving. Cursing, Daphne put herself between the monster and Cross, continuing to fire. She had to distract it, to give Cross a chance to get to safety.

She knew she'd succeeded when the reanimate's dead gaze turned to her. Under other circumstances she might have felt a sense of accomplishment. Now, she felt only abject terror. There was no humanity in that gaze, only mindless malevolence.

Archangel wasn't sure whether they had just suffered a disaster or a divine act of providence. The explosion of the sentry balloons had caused both power-suited sentries to abandon their routes and move toward the facility at flank speed. They'd been at the ends of the building when the explosion occurred; both chose to make a beeline for the loading dock.

Archangel gave them time to reach the center of the courtyard before he dropped from his tree and raced toward the rear of the building. The power-suits had gotten to the bottom of the loading dock steps when a pile of flaming debris that had snagged atop the roof, tumbled down on to the loading dock, catching it afire.

The power-suits hesitated, then one of them wheeled about suddenly. Its augmented gaze caught Archangel halfway across the courtyard. He dove behind one of the steam lorries, but it was too late; he must have pinged their tracking devices. The first power-suit was already on its way toward him, with the other not far behind. Both lifted their hydraulically powered arms and began firing at him, careless of the lorry. Their charges hit its cargo box and shrapnel flew, narrowly missing Archangel's face mask. He dove again, this time pitching himself beneath the vehicle, where he activated the new energy weapon that Tesla and Bobby had integrated into his left vambrace. When the power-suits had come within ten feet of the lorry, he fired, rolled into the clear and fired again, directly at the lead power-suit.

The shot was true. It caught the armored exo-skeleton in the face-plate, shattering the glass and incinerating the driver. The empty suit froze in place, then sagged slowly toward the ground. But before it had fallen, its cohort had taken up the fight, speeding its advance and firing indiscriminately.

Archangel angled a dive that brought him to his feet directly behind the driverless power-suit. He checked his own armaments; he had several energy shots left at a normal intensity . . . or, he could use all three in one shot three times the amplitude. He dialed up the intensity of the weapon to full, then, using the power-suit as cover, he unleashed his final shot at the oncoming adversary. He hit the manned machine directly at its core, slagging the armor, killing the pilot, and burning straight through to the motor that drove it. The explosion was so powerful, it left only the lower legs.

Aware that he was down to more mundane weaponry, Archangel dashed for the factory.

The Bellanger woman continued to fire at the reanimated cadaver, though her shots were doing little more than tearing holes in the thing and angering it further.

Mordecai Judd gritted his teeth. If she were not skittering backward across the lab floor, if she could but get to a safe place and take aim, she might blow its head off. He saw her glance at the energy gauge on her pistol. Judging by the twist of her mouth, she had few shots left and still the creature came at her, its mouth agape and bellowing like a maddened bull.

Mordecai pulled his own pistol and took careful aim at the cadaver's head. He might have hit it, had a bit of falling balloon fabric not settled on his arm just as he fired. Instead, his shot hit the reanimate in the shoulder, ripping away what was left of the jacket it had been wearing and tearing the grey flesh.

Well, if he'd meant to get the thing's attention, he'd certainly succeeded. It shifted its focus immediately from the Bellanger woman
to Mordecai.

"Damn it all to hell," he growled, watching the monster lurch toward him.

Cross started forward and, for a moment, Mordecai thought he meant
to offer aid. Instead, he grabbed Daphne by the arm and hauled her back
toward the lab doors.

"We're under attack!" he shouted, as if that was not the most obvious
fact in the world. "We've got to get to the Comms room! Let's go!" He
turned and fled back toward the eastern wing of the facility, dragging the
bloody woman along with him.

Damn you! Mordecai roared inwardly. He didn't dare take his eyes off the
creature, which made escape difficult. In the next moment, he found escape
was impossible; trying to reach the steps up into the gallery—where he
might at least put the barrier railing between himself and the enraged
brute—he backed into one of von Brant's machines. It was solid and evi-
dently bolted to the floor. It didn't so much as quiver when he rammed his
back against it.

He shot a fevered glance to where he thought the steps should
be. That was all the opportunity the rampaging cadaver needed. It
lurched forward and grasped Mordecai in its huge hands, lifting him
from the floor as if he did not weigh twenty-two stone, and tossing
him halfway across the lab. He hit the gallery rail, but instead of tumbling over it to relative safety, he bounced back and landed face first
on the concrete floor. He saw the heavy-booted feet draw near as the
thing moved in to finish him off.

With a shout and a blur of movement, Iron Rail Jack came out of
nowhere and leapt aboard the great brute as if to take a piggy back
ride. He got a long forearm around the thing's neck and began to
squeeze.

Mordecai had no idea what effect that would have, but he hoped
it was enough of a distraction to allow him to get to one of the energy rifles that lay, unmanned, on the floor near the operating table.
Cursing the pain in his back and jaw, he scrambled to the soot spot

that marked where one of the hapless lab technicians had been, picked up the fallen rifle, then turned to see how Jack was faring.

Not well. His fellow reanimate had more than ten stone on him and a greater mass, making their wrestling match one-sided. Even as Mordecai approached, the abomination threw Jack over his head and slammed him to the floor.

A maniacal grin seized the cadaver's face as it raised a booted foot over Jack's head.

"Hey!" snarled Mordecai. "Hey, you!"

The creature lowered its foot and turned, face twisting into a rictus of rage. It found itself face to muzzle with Mordecai's pulse rifle.

The pirate lord smiled. "Cheers," he said, and pulled the trigger.

The blast from the rifle was enough to take the monster's head clean off its beefy shoulders. It staggered backward for a moment, reflexively lifting its hands to where its head had been, then keeled over backward, hitting the lab floor with a thud.

Mordecai took a deep breath and closed his eyes. He opened them when he heard a cackle of laughter to his right. Jack had gotten to his feet and capered over to the body of the fallen reanimate where he danced a bit of a jig. He stopped to grin at Mordecai.

"Just like old times, aye, Captain?"

Mordecai found himself grinning right back. Nothing like a close brush with death to make a man feel alive. He heard his own pulse in his ears, felt his blood singing through his veins, felt laughter building up inside him. He let the laughter out in a single cracking guffaw, then looked around at the ruined lab.

Someone was missing.

"Did von Brant take Tesla?"

"No sir. I had him right up until I saw that thing was about to commit murder on you. Had to let go of him then."

Mordecai nodded. They had what they needed from the foreign scientist. Chances were good they could do without him.

"Well, my man," he told Jack, "he's probably rabbited right out of here. But, given the situation, I'm personally glad you let him go."

He hefted the rifle. "Let's go see what's become of our fearless leader, shall we?"

Jack gave him a saucy salute. "Aye, sir. After you."

Mordecai gave the headless corpse one last look, then led the way toward the Comms room.

EIGHTEEN -
AN EXPLOSIVE SITUATION

ENFIELD

L ISTENING TO THE SOUND OF SPORADIC GUNFIRE, MACKENZIE Graham flattened himself against the wall of the factory, peered through the broad warehouse doorway behind the loading dock, and took stock of the situation. The dock itself was a shambles; the wooden extension had burnt almost entirely away and the concrete platform that extended outside the doors of the warehouse was covered with soot. Alas, the munitions in the warehouse itself were barely touched, which meant he would have to make sure they perished spectacularly himself . . . once he'd gotten past the Legionnaires who were firing from farther back in the deep, narrow room.

He was certain they were defending the stockpile of weapons, and he suspected that stockpile lay just on the other side of a barn door in the right hand wall roughly two-thirds of the way to the rear of the warehouse. Thick, and as tall as it was wide, it hung from an iron wheel set into a metal track.

He checked his knapsack and turned back to face the team of commandos he led. "Cover me," he said.

The moment they opened fire, aiming high, he went low, rolling around the door jamb before flinging himself behind a pile of crates. A spatter of bullets traced his path. Crouching, he continued around the perimeter of the room as his men drew the enemy's fire. He heard a couple of the Legion soldiers cry out and their weapons clatter to the floor. The Resistance fighters were good. A couple of his men and women were ex-cavalry and could fire with stunning accuracy even from horseback or steam carriage. Their aim when not in motion was even more spectacular. The youngest of them, Brewster Thompson, was a dead shot, and Kenzie would be willing to bet he'd taken out at least one of the Legion minions.

He negotiated the corner and started up the right hand wall toward the barn door that most certainly opened into the main munitions stockpile. He stopped behind a rack of rifles and peered through the long barrels toward the depot doorway. About four feet in front of the door, a pair of Legion soldiers were hunkered behind a some half-packed crates, their eyes riveted on the loading dock. He took them both out with two shots, then swore eloquently as the inner doors at the rear of the warehouse opened inward and another half-dozen Legionnaires dashed through them.

He spoke urgently into his comms transmitter. "Hold them off as long as you can!" he told his second, then he made a quick visual sweep of the room and streaked the last six feet to the barn door.

A shot of energy to the electromagnetic lock popped it open. He slipped through the door and rolled it shut again, to find himself in a room with massive stacks of ordnance crates and rack after rack of weaponry— some of which he'd never seen the like of before.

"Oh, murder," he whispered.

The temptation to snag one of the strange new weapons for Bobby to study almost seduced him, but he tamped the urge down and moved to the center of the room where he knelt and swung his knapsack from his back. As he did, he glanced back the way he'd come.

Odd. The far wall was closer than he'd expected. Judging from the outside dimensions of the building, there ought to be a lot more to this wing. He straightened, wondering what was on the other side of that wall, and caught sight of an open archway leading into yet another chamber.

"Oh, *bloody* murder."

Shouldering his pack again, he moved in that direction, heart rate accelerating in anticipation of what he'd see. Before he even reached the archway, he began to appreciate the sheer magnitude of what lay beyond—a second stockpile even larger than the one in which he stood and replete with unmanned power-suits and other large mechanisms, some with wheels and some with treads. And there were mines, too, and energy cannon. And, of course, there was ordnance for all of it. It was like a warmonger's garden—each little patch growing its own hideous fruit and flower.

Kenzie sucked in a deep breath, unsure whether to celebrate or rue the sudden expansion of his target. He opted for raw determination. He had a finite set of charges to set here; he had to save a few for the lab. He decided he'd best be about figuring where they'd do the most good . . . or bad, as the case may be.

He settled on the largest crates of the most powerful ordnance he could see and lifted a charge out of his pack. Good for a start. From here he'd move to the mines, then make his way back toward the warehouse, where he hoped his team was in the process of cleaning house.

One by one, he pulled out the timed charges Bobby had made and attached each one to a crate of ordnance, beginning with the pumpkin-sized charge packs for the energy cannons. The warning stenciled on the side of each huge crate made him chuckle: EXPLOSIVES - HIGHLY VOLATILE - NO SMOKING.

"I should hope they're highly volatile," he murmured. If all went as might be expected, this place would go up in an explosion that would gut this entire wing of the building.

Having set all the charges, Kenzie went swiftly back along his trail to each one, flipping the toggle that would start the clock. Then he headed back to the warehouse.

Ginny Gelson had brought her team in through the north entrance at the rear of the east wing of the facility, far away from the chaos caused by the overhead explosions. They were traversing what looked like a residential wing in the maze-like interior and had just come across a large kitchen. Ginny was hopeful that the bulk of the Legion's defensive forces had been deployed to protect the munitions depot and labs at the opposite end of the building. So far her hopes had been realized. They'd come across no one in their travels so far.

She led her team to the far side of the kitchen and out through a set of doors big enough for a carriage house. In fact, they rather looked like carriage house doors—thick and hung from an over head track on a metal wheel. On the other side of the doors they found a large, high-ceilinged room. It was dark; the only light filtered in from the kitchen. By aid of that meager illumination, Ginny could see the room was filled with crates, boxes, and sacks. Wine bottles poked out of one crate, a stack of dishes sat atop another. Apparently the large storage room had been repurposed into a pantry for provisions. There were food smells here, mingled with other, less identifiable odors.

"Lights," she murmured, moving to activate the small electric lamp strapped to her forearm.

A companion's light flashed on in the periphery of her vision and, suddenly, the place was alive with gunfire. She heard the cries of at least two of her commandos as they were cut down by hidden snipers.

"Trap! Down! *Down!*" Ginny dropped to the floor and rolled for cover.

Bullets and energy bolts continued to fly, hitting indiscriminately and sending splinters, glass, and pottery debris in all directions. Some of the large sacks, breached by the barrage, belched billows of flour into the air, creating clouds of the stuff that added to the chaos.

Ginny and her team returned fire. From her position, to the right of the kitchen doors, she could just make out a second set of doors on the far side of the room. This was where the enemy fire originated. Clearly, the Legion did not want her going through those doors.

Well, now, if that was the case, she was most definitely going through them. End of story.

She was considering how best to achieve that seemingly impossible goal, when she caught movement above and to her right. She peered upward, realizing that the ceiling was much higher than she had first thought, and that there was a catwalk around at least a portion of the room at a height of roughly ten feet. In the fitful bursts of weapons fire, Ginny saw a sight that steadied her pulse and put a grin on her face. Archangel was up on the catwalk, making his way along it behind the Legion snipers.

"Keep it up, boys!" she shouted to her team. "Give 'em hell!"

The commandos redoubled their effort, lighting up the room as if it had been full of fireworks instead of provisions. Ginny, still firing, watched Archangel's progress along the catwalk. When he was directly above the center of the Legion team, he made a cutting gesture at Ginny.

"*Hold fire!*" she cried.

It took a moment for the Legionnaires to realize their adversaries had stopped shooting at them. Their shots slackened, too. Ginny could imagine what their leader was thinking: *Have they escaped back the way they came? Should we pursue?*

In that moment of uncertainty, Archangel dropped down from above. In the dim light from the kitchen, Ginny saw him draw his sword, its blade flashing silver. Two of the Legion troopers half rose from concealment, their weapons raised, but silent. The quarters were too tight to fire; they would have to resort to close combat—and there, Archangel had the advantage. His sword flashed again and again, and though they tried to block it with their rifles, Legionnaires fell until none rose to fight.

Ginny waited, gun trained on the far side of the room, until Archangel gave the all-clear. Then she and her team rose from concealment and met him in the center of the large chamber.

"Did you see anyone on your way in?" he asked, his voice distorted slightly by the filters in his face mask.

"No, sir. Not a soul."

"We have to find Tesla and get out of here," he told her. "There've been some unexpected complications in and around the lab, but I'm hoping Kenzie will be able to blow the ordnance as planned." He gestured back over his shoulder. "We can't get out that way; there'll be more of them coming. We'd best circle around the perimeter and make a thorough check of the quarters on this side in the event that's where they've stashed Tesla. We'll go back the way you came in."

Ginny gave him a wry smile. "Through the servants' entrance?"

"Ginny!" said one of the commandos nearest the kitchen doors. "D'you hear that?"

'That' was the rapidly growing sound of mechanical thumping that could only be—

"Power-suits!" Ginny cried.

She whirled toward the kitchen doors, but before she could raise her weapon, that route was blocked by two of the metal-clad warriors. They ducked to enter the room, accompanied by a handful of Legion reinforcements, their weapons already trained on Ginny and her companions. In moments, the Resistance fighters were surrounded.

Ginny looked to Archangel. She supposed she expected him to do something brilliant and heroic. Perhaps he would have done, but someone else beat him to the punch. Ginny had no more than raised her hands in surrender when an explosion erupted behind the power-suits, violently enlarging the doorway and felling the nearest of their unarmored comrades. The power-suits turned unsteadily to face the new threat.

That, and the billowing smoke, allowed Ginny and her cohorts to drop to the floor and seek cover. When the smoke cleared, there was a man standing in the shattered doorway. A man in commando gear, with a portable energy generator strapped to his back and armed with two bolt rifles so imposing Ginny would have called them cannon.

She knew that face. There wasn't a Resistance fighter who didn't.

Sir Florian Buckingham stepped into the room with a roar. "For Queen and Country!" he shouted, and unleashed a series of energy strikes from his two guns into both power-suits simultaneously. They might as well have been wearing papier-mâché armor for all the good it did them. They were quite literally blown away.

A team of six Paladins—each wearing a smaller version of the brigadier's generator—stormed through the ruined doorway, their own considerable weapons at the ready. They opened fire on what was left of the Legion troops, taking mere seconds to eliminate them.

When it was over, Ginny and the remainder of her team stood and surveyed the wreckage. With clouds of smoke and flour still drifting about them, Buckingham stepped forward to stand face to face with Archangel.

"Brigadier Florian Buckingham reporting for duty, sir." Seeing Ginny standing there agape, he lifted one of his rifles in salute and nodded. "Ma'am."

"Brigadier," said Archangel. The vocal filters in his mask could not conceal his amazement. "It will be my honor to fight with you this day."

Buckingham surveyed the strength of the forces in the room—his six men, Ginny and her strike team of five, Archangel.

"What's the plan?" he asked.

Archangel nodded back toward the doors he'd just liberated from their defenders. "Charges are being set to blow this place to hell. If my man has done his job, we've got less than twenty minutes to find Tesla and get out of here."

"Well, then, I suggest we get moving."

"Back the way you came," said Archangel. "This side seems to house living quarters. Tesla may be here somewhere, and I intend to find him."

Gunfire seemed to come from everywhere—both the loud, sharp report of ballistic weapons and the strange, sizzling shock of energy rifles. Daphne had once watched a house burn—a house she had lived in. The din energy weapons made was very like the sound of fire sucking oxygen and life out of a wooden building as it sagged toward oblivion.

In the chaos of the journey, she kept her attention focused on Benton Cross as they fled through the dark warren of hallways and rooms with Dr. von Brant. They were in what had been the management offices of the old mill on the top floor of the wing that had housed Cross's staff and troops.

It had come to her, as they zig-zagged through the corridors, that though her gun had been useless against von Brant's monstrosity, she might have at any time drawn her saber and cut off its head, or lopped off its arms—though she'd've had to get within arms' reach, herself, to do so. But she had been distracted—so worried for Benton Cross's welfare, that she had ceased to think like a warrior and begun to think like a lover. As anathema to her as that was—as inexcusable as Cross, himself, might have found it—was it possible that it was her thinking like his lover that had saved his life?

She expected she'd never know.

They turned a corner into a short hallway that ran across the back of the eastern wing of the building and she saw their destination—an open door with a brass placard that declared it the Communications Room.

Daphne took charge, slipping past her companions, rushing into the little office, and seating herself at the controls of a communications console. It seemed horribly out of place in this antique of a building, its dials and switches and running lights looking modern and precise against the aging brick of the walls and the worn desk on which it sat.

She set aside her useless pistol and flipped a series of switches to the "on" position. Lights went from yellow to green, prompting her to use one of the dials to find the frequency on which Cross's air fleet sent and received transmissions. Finding it, she pulled the speaking diaphragm toward her and spoke urgently into it.

"Enfield One to *War Raven*. Come in, *War Raven*." She paused, but there was no response; there was not even static. Dear God, had the Resistance somehow taken out their warships, too? "Enfield One to *War Raven*," she repeated. "Come in, *War Raven*."

There was a crackle of static at last, then: "This is Captain Grant of the *War Raven*, Enfield One, over."

Daphne opened her mouth to order Grant to come in, but Cross ripped the communications device from her hands and snarled into it.

"This is Benton Cross. The Enfield facility is under attack by Resistance forces. We need air support and an air lift out of here. Now!"

"Understood, Mr. Cross. We estimate we can be there in three minutes."

Daphne saw the muscles in Cross's jaw bunch in frustration, but he took a deep breath and schooled his voice.

"Excellent, Captain. Meet us at the rear of the eastern wing. And ready your weapons, Mr. Grant. Be prepared for a fight."

"What manner of forces, sir? What is their strength?"

"I don't know. Be prepared for anything. Do your duty, Mr. Grant. Get. Us. Out of here. Cross, out."

Nineteen - Ether

With Archangel in the lead, the Resistance forces traversed a corridor lined with doors that opened into living quarters, common rooms, still rooms, and the occasional water closet. They moved as swiftly as they could while still checking each room for the kidnapped scientist. They were on the premier floor of the east wing and had just turned into a cross corridor that ran the length of the building's core, when someone stepped out into the hall in front of them.

Archangel raised his energy pistol, but Ginny put a hand to his arm to stay him.

"Sir! It's Kenzie!" she cried. She let out a chuff of air, then added, "The man is an irritant, but useful. Shooting him would be counter-productive."

"Lord, are you a sight for sore eyes," Kenzie said, moving down the hall toward them.

Three more Resistance commandos appeared from the cross corridor and hastened after him. Ginny's heart fell. Only three? How many good people were they to lose today?

"How did it go, Kenzie?" Archangel asked.

The young Scot grimaced. "We lost Williams and Beckett. *But*, the charges on the munitions have been set. Should take out most of the western wing. We need to set the last few in the lab area, though, just in case the depot goin' up doesn't do the trick. We tried to get into the lab from the other side, but couldn't get through. So, we came up this way, figuring to go over on a higher floor, then back down." His gaze shifted to Buckingham. "Good to see you, Brigadier. Glad you still enjoy a good fight."

Buckingham gave him a wry nod.

"We've yet to find Tesla," said Archangel. "But right now we need to prioritize blowing the lab and getting the hell out of here." He turned to Buckingham. "Brigadier, can you and your men clear us a path from here to the rear entrance of the east wing?"

Buckingham nodded. "Consider it done, sir."

Archangel turned his attention to Ginny next. "Ginny, take your men and Kenzie's and go with the brigadier. Keep an eye out for the good professor."

Ginny opened her mouth to protest that she wanted to be in the heart of the battle, but instead asked, "What do *you* intend to do, sir?"

"I'll accompany Kenzie. We won't be far behind you."

Ginny swallowed her disappointment . . . and, yes, her fear. If they lost even the annoying Scotsman, they'd be set back tremendously. If they lost Archangel . . . .

"Yes, sir," she murmured.

"Don't worry, luv," Kenzie said drily. "You'll be seein' me again."

Under normal circumstances, she'd have rolled her eyes or turned her back on him and walked away. These were not normal circumstances, so she did nothing.

Kenzie nodded at Archangel, and the two men turned to head out.

"God speed, sir," said Buckingham. "We'll be waiting for you."

Archangel sketched a salute at his ex-commander, then he and Kenzie ran side by side into the heart of the building.

The brigadier stepped into the command role instantly. "Let's move it, boys," he said, then slanted a sideways glance at Ginny. "Miss. There's a pint waiting for each of you in London, or a cup of tea if you prefer."

"I'll take the pint," said Ginny and followed Buckingham back into the east wing.

Mordecai would not have admitted it in a thousand years, but he was beginning to think he was lost in the seemingly endless warren of corridors and rooms and anonymous caverns that made up the Enfield facility. From the lab, he and Iron Rail Jack had climbed to the first floor where Mordecai expected to find far fewer skirmishes going on. He'd been right, as it happened, but the moment they set foot back on the ground floor, they were fired upon by a group of Rezzies that included two SIS Paladins. He'd no idea there were any Paladins left alive, yet there they were, clad in their dark uniforms, but with their faces half-covered with some sort of goggles.

"With me!" Mordecai shouted, and dove through the nearest doorway into one of the barracks rooms that housed Legion staff and troops. The room was empty, its inhabitants having scrambled to repel the attackers. He rolled behind an iron bedstead with Jack close behind.

The two men fired round after round through the open doorway, Mordecai ducking when shots from the Rezzies struck too close. Occasionally, a shot would hit one of the beds, spewing mattress stuffing or splinters everywhere.

"You know," the warlord observed, as he reloaded his pistol, "*you've* nothing to fear from these blokes. You might consider marching out there and taking them out."

"Nothing to fear?" laughed Jack. "Sir, did the way you killed that brute in the lab teach you nothing? If I were to be hit with enough energy bolts— or just one in the right place at the right range, I doubt me mam could stitch me back together right, and she were the best seamstress in Hull. I'll be staying right here, I think."

"Well then, rather than waste ammo . . . ."

Mordecai stopped firing. After a moment, so did Jack. As Mordecai had anticipated, it wasn't long before one of the commandos issued forth to see if perhaps they'd managed to dispatch their target. When he did, Mordecai took him out with one shot.

Jack was all admiration. "You still got the eye, Cap. You still got the dead eye."

Mordecai came close to observing that it was Jack who literally had dead eyes, but decided against it. Instead, he merely said, "That's only one down, mate. And I doubt these boys will fall for the same trick twice." He considered the lay of the room. "Cover me," he ordered, and rolled across the aisle between rows of beds to the opposite side of the room while Jack lay down a volley of cover. Then, he wriggled forward to the bed closest to the door. From this vantage point, he could see enough of one Paladin that he was able to deal him a shot to the shoulder. The man wasn't dead, but he was down. If he'd counted right, that left two more—possibly three.

"You know," Mordecai said between shots, "this reminds me of the time we were pinned down during the prison break in Manchester."

Jack let out a bark of laughter that sounded like the creaking of a rusty hinge. "Yeah! You remember what we did there, do you?"

"I do, Jack. Just give the word."

Jack stopped shooting for a moment while Mordecai continued to fire. The Red Tong warlord knew what his lieutenant was doing—counting shots, watching for the source of bolt flashes. After a time he began firing again, but lifted a hand and gave his captain a signal: two fingers and a gesture to the left; one finger and a gesture to the right.

Three, then. Mordecai nodded.

"Now!" cried Jack, and both men came up out of their hiding spots with guns and mouths roaring, firing diagonally across the open doorway.

Mordecai focused his entire attention on the one man to the right; Jack concentrated on the two to the left. As it had done in their prison break, the crazy maneuver caught the remaining fighters off-guard. All three were cut down, though Jack suffered a hole in his disreputable coat and a small missing piece of the thigh it had been covering. The wounded Paladin had apparently fled, for there was no sign of him. A shame. He was likely to carry tales to his commander, whoever that was. Mordecai had his suspicions.

Surveying the corpses, Mordecai chuckled, shaking his head. "That crazy shit still works!"

Jack, laughing with him, walked over to lay a hand on his shoulder. "Sorry, Captain, but in all of the confusion, I forgot to give you something I think you'll be happy to see."

The reanimate reached into his coat pocket and withdrew a small wooden box—the same wooden box whose contents Cross had been admiring in the lab. Mordecai took it, feeling something like awe. He glanced at Jack's grinning face, then slowly slid back the little wooden lid. Breath stopped in his lungs. Inside the box, cradled in a velvet lining, were three glass and steel vials containing a clear blue liquid that seemed to glow with its own light. In a row above the vials were six shiny metal disks, each the size of a pence. Mordecai felt his lips pull back in a Cheshire Cat smile.

"How did you ever get these?"

"Oh," said Jack, looking very pleased with himself, "let's just say that Mr. Cross became a bit distracted what with all the hullaballoo in the lab. He misplaced his little box and I just figured he'd be mighty happy if I were to make sure it come out alive, as it were. *You're* mighty happy, aren't you, Cap?"

Mordecai nodded. "Oh, yes, my friend. Mighty happy."

He closed the box, double-checking that it was securely fastened, then slipped it into an inner pocket of his cutaway coat.

"C'mon, Jack. We'd best move before we have to do the Manchester maneuver yet again."

He led the way toward the north entrance to the east wing, where the corner of the building came closest to the concealing forest. The sun would rise soon and he didn't want to be caught in the open when that happened.

Cross was all for descending to the ground floor to wait for the War Raven to appear; Daphne argued for remaining on the upper floor in the Comms room, which was in the inner corner of the east wing and had windows on two sides. The north-facing windows looked out on the grounds and the woodland; the west-facing ones afforded a view of the courtyard at the rear of the building and the western wing.

"Here, we're safest," she insisted. "And here, we can see farther. When the ship comes, we'll know it far sooner if we stay aloft and descend only at the last moment."

To illustrate her point, she made a sweeping west-to-east gesture, noticing as she did that the landscape outside was turning from black to purple-grey. Sunrise would be sooner than perhaps they wished. She was about to suggest they try to locate a set of field glasses, when she spied something—or, rather, some*one*—peering from a ground floor window at the back of the central wing of the facility.

She smiled grimly. "Well, now. I think I've just found our missing scientist."

Twenty - Dead Men's Tales

ARCHANGEL AND KENZIE ARRIVED AT THE LABORATORY TO FIND
it deserted—an island of stillness in the chaos going on in other
parts of the immense facility. That there had been chaos here
earlier was obvious from the state of the chamber. Charred spots
smudged what should have been pristine surfaces. Shattered glass and
fallen bits of ceiling littered the floor. Among the debris were abandoned weapons, the bodies of dead technicians, and the wreckage of
the operating table.

"Murder," breathed Kenzie, touching a finger to the edge of one of
the table's torn restraints. "This bloody thing is near half an inch thick, but
it's torn like . . . ."

"Like something immensely strong but with no fear of pain rent it?"
asked Archangel.

He paused in scanning for the best places to set their charges and
nodded toward the headless hulk of a reanimate lying beneath the gallery
rail. It was easily recognizable by the mottled grey of its exposed
flesh.

Kenzie followed his gaze and winced. "Aye. Like that."

"Let's split up. We don't have much time. Toss me some of the charges."

Kenzie nodded, reached into his rucksack, and lobbed a couple of the
inert charges to his commander. Archangel caught the small devices and

slipped behind the bank of controls near the operating table, seeking a vulnerable point.

"I'll just go decorate those machines on the other side of the room," Kenzie said.

His steps crossed the cement floor and tapped the metal stairs as he ran lightly up into the low gallery to begin setting charges there.

"Funny, isn't it," he said as he worked, "how scientists' lairs always seem to have the same basic design—a central theater and a gallery from which the adoring acolytes can watch the genius at work." He said the words "theater" and "gallery" with an extra measure of drama.

Archangel, intent on placing his bombs swiftly and well, didn't reply, so Kenzie—being Kenzie—continued to chatter.

"I wonder if Artemus was thinking along those lines when he designed *his* lab. After all—" He cut off and gave a muted cough.

Archangel felt a tingle of alarm run up his spine a split second before Benton Cross's voice froze him.

"Archangel! Step slowly from behind that machine with your hands raised. Do it now, or I will kill your pathetic comrade."

Archangel set his second charge and moved out into the open, facing toward the sound of Cross's voice. The Legion warlord was up on the gallery at the far end of the room with von Brant on his left. On his right, Daphne Bellanger held Kenzie in a chokehold, the blade of her sword pressed to his neck.

"I'd suggest you don't come any closer," she warned, "or your little Scottish naif here may be performing his morning hymn with a choir of angels."

Archangel flicked his augmented gaze from the woman to her master. He felt cold to the core. "Let him go, Cross. Your fight is with me, not him."

"No, no, no. My fight is with anyone who is an enemy of the Legion. I won't rest until the Resistance is crushed and every last one of you is dead."

"Trust me, the feeling is entirely mutual."

"Of course it is. Now, drop your weapons."

Archangel complied, letting his pistol and saber clatter to the floor. His left vambrace weapon was spent and, though the right one was still outfitted with an energy pulse generator, it took precious and noisy seconds to build up a charge—seconds he didn't have. He flexed his hands futilely and surveyed his immediate surroundings for a weapon of opportunity, knowing his mask concealed the movement of his eyes. On the tray next to the operating table was a nasty-looking awl or screwdriver. It would be within arm's reach if he lunged a bit to his left.

"You really don't have time for this, Cross," he said, as he used a twist of his right wrist to drop one of Bobby's little smoke bombs into the palm of his gloved hand.

"Really? And why is that?"

"Because this place is set to go off like a powder keg in about five minutes. What did you think we were doing here, having tea?"

He pressed the timer and flicked the smoke bomb into the middle of the lab floor. It exploded in an impenetrable cloud of dark smoke that filled the large space in seconds. At least it was impenetrable to anyone not wearing heat-sensing lenses like the ones in Archangel's optics.

He lunged to his left, caught up the awl and flung it at the orange-red shape he knew was Benton Cross. Cross let out a roar of pain as the thing embedded itself in his shoulder. Archangel continued to his left, hoping to come at his adversaries from an unexpected angle. He could see Kenzie's profile with the aide of his lenses—an oddly pale ghost-figure that was even now pulling away from the Bellanger woman.

She let him go and spun toward Cross. "We have to get out of here! Now!" she cried.

"He's lying!" roared Cross. "They'd never destroy—"

"We can't take that chance!"

Through the billowing smoke, Archangel saw Cross wrench the awl from his shoulder, staggering backward to follow von Brant from the lab. Bellanger grasped his good arm and hauled him toward the doors that led to the eastern wing. He started to go with her, then hesitated. He turned back into the lab, pulled a gun from beneath his coat and aimed it at Kenzie.

Archangel realized too late that it was an energy weapon. A brilliant bolt shot from the muzzle, hitting Kenzie squarely in the chest. He was flung backward against the plate-metal of the machine he'd been sabotaging, hitting it with a solid impact that made the metal ring like a bell.

Cross let Bellanger hustle him from the room. Archangel didn't consider pursuing him for an instant. He raced for the gallery, shouting Kenzie's name. By the time he reached the younger man, he had slid to the metal floor, his head propped up against the machine. Archangel dropped down beside him, reaching gloved hands out to examine his wound. Kenzie weakly pushed his hands away.

"Go after them, sir," he panted. "Don't worry 'bout me. We don't have much time and we can't let them get away."

"I don't care if they get away. The only way I'm leaving here is with you. Hold on, Kenzie. Hold on for me."

The words had no more than left his lips, than Archangel saw a figure weaving its way toward them through the chemical fog. He tensed, aware that the short distance between himself and his fallen weapons might as well be a mile.

"Dear God!" said a familiar voice, and Nikola Tesla appeared out of the thinning smoke. "What happened?"

"Cross happened. Can you help him?"

Kenzie's eyes had closed and his breath was coming in uneven gasps. Tesla knelt beside him, the look on his face one of amazement.

"It's *you!*" he breathed. "How can it be you?"

Archangel shook his head, feeling confusion-laced anguish building up in his soul. "What do you mean? Is it who? What is it, Doctor?"

Instead of answering his question, Tesla leapt to his feet and launched himself from the gallery down the steps into the lab. He made a beeline for the operating table, where he conducted a frantic search of the tray next to the helm.

"He's dying, damn you!" roared Archangel.

Tesla made an inarticulate sound of triumph, then sprinted back to the gallery, the diminishing fog roiling and billowing in his wake. In his hands was what looked like a tiny wooden suitcase. He dropped to his knees next to Kenzie, set the little case on the Scotsman's chest and flipped open the unmarked lid. Inside was some sort of miniature machine comprised of a small console with a dial, a gauge, and two round metal connectors attached to the console by slender wires.

"What are you doing?" Archangel asked. "What is that?"

"Just help me. Lift his head away from that metal panel."

Archangel started to do as asked, then realized that his young friend had gone completely limp, his skin wearing the grey pall of death. He took a deep breath; his lungs suddenly seemed too small.

"It's too late, professor."

"Nonsense," said Tesla briskly. "You have no idea."

He shoved the connectors into Archangel's hands, then shifted Kenzie's head from the metal plating to prop it on his right knee. With long, delicate fingers, he combed the young Scotsman's longish hair back from his temples. There, embedded in the skin just above his sideburns, were two very small metal discs.

"Your gloves will protect you from the current," said Tesla as if he were speaking to a small child. "Hold one of these connectors on each of those receptors. Quickly, sir. Time is of the essence."

In more ways than one, Archangel thought, as he pressed the connectors to Kenzie's temples. He might have exaggerated how much urgency was needed for Cross's benefit, but every second they tarried here, was a second closer to a fiery death.

Tesla flipped a switch on the little console, counted quietly to ten, then turned the dial. There was a hum of electrical power and Archangel felt the connectors he held vibrate even through his shielded gloves. Kenzie's body went suddenly rigid, his back arching, his limbs going stiff and straight. His eyes flew open to stare at the ceiling overhead.

Tesla shut the little machine down, while Archangel could do no more than stare at MacKenzie Graham, who was now staring back at him in obvious confusion.

"Are you . . . ?" Archangel cleared his throat. "Are you all right?"

The younger man frowned as if trying to process what had happened. "I think I am. Yes. But honestly, I thought I'd wake up dead. Why did I not wake up dead?"

Archangel nodded at Tesla. "You've the professor to thank for that."

"Thank you, professor," murmured Kenzie. "Thank you for my life."

"No time for niceties," Archangel reminded him. "Your time bombs are nearly done ticking. Can you walk?"

"I'll do you one better. I think I can run. And I suggest we do."

Archangel and Tesla pulled Kenzie to his feet and the trio raced from the lab as fast as their legs would carry them.

TWENTY-ONE - RIGHT-HAND MAN

MORDECAI JUDD PEERED UP FROM BENEATH THE EAVES AT THE back of the factory's east wing. Overhead, the dark bulk of a Legion warship loomed as she maneuvered above the open field behind the building. The pictogram painted on her canopy announced that she was the *War Raven*, Benton Cross's flagship.

"Well, Jack," Mordecai told his companion, "it looks as if our chariot has arrived."

As the two skyraiders watched, the ship turned her starboard flank parallel to the building and dropped a pair of rope ladders.

"Ah! She's right on time."

Benton Cross stepped out into the rear vestibule with his woman and pet scientist in tow. Blood stained the left shoulder of his jacket and he'd thrust his hand into his pocket to steady his arm. Clearly his passage to safety had not been even as uneventful as Mordecai's. Von Brant, the cowering old fool, was weaponless, depending on others to save his sorry self; Bellanger carried a rapid-repeating rifle. The Serbian genius was nowhere to be seen. Apparently, they'd managed to lose him again.

Cross gestured to von Brant. "Up you go, Doctor."

The scientist looked about frantically as if Resistance snipers might be hiding in the bushes (as they might well be), then trundled toward the nearest rope ladder and began to climb.

Cross turned to the woman next, but she put a hand on his arm and shook her head. "You go first, Benton. I'll cover you."

He gave her a strange look. "Daphne! I do believe that's the first time you've ever used my given name."

The twist of her lips was not quite a smile. "We'll be right behind you. I want to make sure you get out of here safely."

Cross touched her cheek briefly, nodded, and raced to the second ladder, his gait uneven due to his wounded shoulder. Even with only one arm to aid in his climb, he was faster than the German.

"Who did that to him?" Mordecai asked. "Just out of curiosity."

"Archangel," Bellanger snarled. "I swear sometimes that man is supernatural."

"That thought had crossed my mind, as well," admitted Mordecai, watching Cross's progress up the ladder.

"As much as I'd like to stay and chat," said Iron Rail Jack, "I'd say we best sling our arses out of here."

He stepped out into the yard, Mordecai and Bellanger not far behind. He'd taken no more than three strides when his body was ripped apart by an energy blast that could only have come from a high-powered bolt rifle. The entire lower half of his body was all but disintegrated.

In the wake of the shot, Florian Buckingham appeared from around the western corner of the wing. A half-dozen or more Paladins and Resistance commandos were fanned out behind him.

"That," said Buckingham, "was for Sir Henry."

Damn me, I'm dead, thought Mordecai.

But instead of leveling his rifle at the Red Tong leader, Buckingham gritted his teeth and unloaded one more energy blast into what remained of Iron Rail Jack. At that close range, all that the charge left was sludge and embers.

"And *that* was for Annabel."

Mordecai did not wait for the enemy to recover from his moment of vengeance or for his companion to open fire, he spun back into the building, drawing his own weapon. On the opposite side of the doorway, the Bellanger woman had done the same. They'd barely gotten out of sight when they were under fire. Their return fire forced the Resistance warriors to seek cover.

Over the whine and sizzle of weapons discharges, Cross's woman shouted at Mordecai to get to the airship.

"I'm going to lay down cover for you, Captain. Use it to get to the ladder."

Mordecai gave her a glance. "Yes'm. I do believe I can do that."

She let out a scream of rage and began to fire as fast as her gun would allow. It hadn't the raw power of Buckingham's bolt rifle, but it fired faster than humanly possible. As the enemy hunkered out of reach of her bullets, Mordecai streaked across the open ground, hurdling the remains of his lieutenant and making a flying leap up onto the closest ladder. He twisted about, pulling his gun and laying down a pattern of shots that forced the enemy—several of which he could see quite well from his perch—deeper into hiding. They stopped firing altogether, allowing Cross's girlfriend-cum-bodyguard to make her own bid for safety.

When she was well on her way, Mordecai stopped firing and climbed as if the demons of hell were nipping at his boots. He was over halfway up the ladder when the woman reached the bottom of it. She looked up at him, a smile starting to tug at the corners of her mouth.

That smile gave her an advantage over him, Mordecai realized, when it came to procuring a high place in Benton Cross's kingdom. Cross looked at the Red Tong captain as a henchman, an attack dog, a vassal king from a subjugated territory. Mordecai wanted more than that. He wanted to be a Legion warlord in his own right and Benton Cross's right-hand man. Daphne Bellanger—in line to be Benton Cross's queen—stood in his way.

As she began to ascend the ladder, Mordecai lowered his rifle until it was aimed at her heart. She stopped, her smile slipping toward puzzlement. He cocked his head apologetically.

"Sorry and all that," he said, and pulled the trigger.

The blast hit her squarely in the chest and flung her to the ground where she lay, limbs akimbo, like a broken doll. Mordecai turned and continued up the ladder to safety, feeling wind in his face as the *War Raven* began to heel away from the factory.

Florian Buckingham signaled his troops to cease fire and came from cover to watch the Legion warship move way over the trees at flank speed. In moments she was out of range of even his bolt rifle. He moved to stand over the young woman who'd been reduced before his eyes to human wreckage. In the stillness of death, her face had relaxed into an incongruous innocence as if she were an angel flung down from heaven.

"Is she dead, Brigadier?" asked Ginny from behind him.

Yes, she was dead—dead beyond recall, her heart all but blown from her body. He took a deep breath, feeling nothing but a profound weariness.

"Yes, Ginny. Quite dead. So much for honor among thieves."

"Brigadier!"

Buckingham turned at the sound of Brenden Winter's altered voice and saw Archangel step from the factory with his man MacKenzie and the Serbian scientist in tow.

Archangel nodded skyward. "I take it that skyship is where Cross and his minions have gone?"

"Yes. All but this unfortunate woman. She was murdered in cold blood by one of her own." Buckingham looked up at the group of Resistance personnel and Paladins who were emerging from concealment, then turned to Archangel. "Follow us out of here. We'll keep you covered. Most of the Legion soldiers seem to have fled, though I suspect some may yet put up a fight."

With the Sun peeking above the treetops as if to see what had transpired while he slept, the group melted into the forest, keeping a careful eye on the Legion warship as it sailed into the bright eastern sky.

Benton Cross stood beside Viktor von Brant on the bridge of the *War Raven*, watching the forest below take on a ruddy glow as the light of the morning Sun lapped over it. A hatch behind him opened and Mordecai Judd stepped onto the bridge. There was a wariness about the man that prickled Cross's senses.

"Where are Daphne and Jack?"

Judd grimaced. "I'm afraid Jack is no longer with us. Buckingham blew him apart with a bolt rifle."

"And Daphne?"

The skyraider shook his head, making the metal fittings in his hair sing mournfully. "Didn't make it, sir. She insisted on being last up the ladder . . . ."

Cross felt something cold and alien claw at his innards. It took him a moment to recognize it as grief.

"NO!" he roared, grief manifesting as rage. "What do you mean? She was right behind us! *What happened?*"

"It was Archangel's men. There was nothing I could do. After they got Jack, she made me go up before her. Truth is, I didn't even see which one of them did it. I just looked back and there she was, lying on the ground, dead. Sorry, sir."

Cross went deep into himself, his vision going dark and red. For a moment, there was nothing in the universe but him and an ice cold rage so kinetic, it seemed to him to be alive.

"I swear I will kill every last one of them," he murmured. "Every. Last. One." He blinked, forcing his vision outward. Forcing himself to breathe. Then he turned to Captain Grant. "Captain, bring us about. Take us back to the factory. If any of them are still in there, I want to blow them back to their Maker."

The captain hesitated for a split second then nodded. "Aye, sir. Mr. Thornhill, bring us about. Adjust course fifty-nine degrees north by north west. Put us broadside to the building at fifty yards distance. Mr. Mason, fix your cannon and prepare to fire."

Both the helmsman and gunnery officer snapped to smartly, their "aye, sirs" spoken in almost perfect unison. The helm answered immediately and the massive skyship came about with deliberate grandeur and sailed back the way she had come. When she had reached the mark her captain had set, Thornhill turned her port side to the factory, as the gunner adjusted his cannon on their gimbals.

Grant turned to Cross. "On your command, sir."

The morning Sun was beginning to filter down through the trees as Archangel and his party circled back to the west to join with the remainder of their forces. The purr of an engine and an immense light-blocking shadow caused him to peer up through the pine boughs to see that the Legion skyship had come about and was heading back toward the factory. He became aware that Florian Buckingham stopped to follow his gaze.

"Good God," said the brigadier. "What is he doing?"

"Revenge?" suggested Archangel. "The dead woman was his second, possibly more than that. I doubt his skyraider friend admitted to killing her."

"Well, whatever he means to do," said Kenzie, pausing to join them, "he'd best do it quick-like." As if to underscore his words, he pulled a pocket watch from his weskit and flipped it open to check the time. He closed the watch, repocketed it and said, "Let the games begin. Four, three, two—"

Before he reached "one," the western wing of the Enfield facility was wracked by a series of explosions so powerful, they literally lifted the tile roof into the air before it was flung away, its debris riding on the surface of a fireball that dwarfed the warship hovering less than 100 yards away.

The laboratory went up moments later, engulfing the vessel in a second ball of flame. Debris shot into the air, grazing the hull of the gondola and peppering the giant canopy with superheated shrapnel. Viewed through the sheltering trees, the skyship appeared as a grisly silhouette half-devoured by giant gouts of flame.

Archangel watched from the safety of the ground, wondering if short-sighted vengeance might accomplish what he had so far failed to do—stop Benton Cross's insatiable quest for power.

Twenty-Two -
Fire and Ice

THE EXPLOSIONS THAT TORE THROUGH THE FACTORY BELOW HAD reached up to seize *War Raven* in violent and fiery hands. She bucked and rolled like a fractious horse while flame boiled beyond the thick glass of her gondola's windows. Von Brant, bleating like a frightened child, was thrown violently to the deck, while Mordecai and Cross grasped for what handholds they could find. The bridge officers' stations were equipped with both foot and handholds intended to protect them from just such turbulence. This was a warship, after all, and a fine one at that. Mordecai clung to a railing, envying Cross a ship of such construction that she could withstand the punishment she was taking.

Over the thunder and fury, Captain Grant shouted orders to his helmsman. "Veer off, Mr. Thornhill! Veer off! Get us out of here!"

If you still can, thought Mordecai, then realized he wasn't really afraid of the great ship going down. He'd escaped worse situations than this one. He'd led a charmed life—possibly due to the fact of his mam being a witch. Benton Cross was damn lucky to have Mordecai Judd in his "court."

Perversely, Benton Cross seemed not to want to escape the flames. He turned on the good captain with wild-eyed fury, screaming obscenities, and questioning both the officer's parentage and his judgement.

"Damn you, you cowardly son of a bitch! What are you doing? They must all die! Have you run mad?"

"I assure you, *I* have not," the captain replied, with subtle emphasis. "We must get out of here now, or we will perish. We've sustained major damage to our port side, and may lose our turbines or our rudder at any moment. If we do not leave now, we may may not make it back to base at all. And I shouldn't have to tell you what will happen if the flames catch on our canopy."

Mordecai watched the play of emotions on the Legion warlord's face with fascination. He was witnessing an elemental battle as the hot and mercurial struggled against something icy and implacable. Ice triumphed over fire . . . this time.

"Very well, Captain," Cross ground out between clenched teeth. Every word sounded as if it had been chewed to shreds before it left his mouth.

The ship was already coming about, leaving the boiling flame for concealing smoke. Cross turned his head to stare out the windows, his knuckles white as he gripped a metal stanchion with his good right hand.

"Another time, Archangel," he murmured. "Another time."

Mordecai could feel Cross's rage and hatred coming off him in waves. He pledged then and there that this man must never know how Daphne Bellanger had really died.

Archangel watched with something like awe as the great Legion warship pulled herself out of the roil of flame and smoke and limped off to the northeast. Even without using his distance lenses, he could see that some of her rigging had been burnt away causing her canopy to bulge unevenly. Her port side was pocked and scorched from stem to stern, her rudder hung crookedly in its brackets, and her port turbines were firing erratically and making noises that indicated their propellers were damaged. Her helmsman would be lucky to hold her to a straight course.

As he turned to look back over his shoulder toward the burning factory, Tesla moved to stand beside him.

"Thank God that evil place is no more," the scientist said with much feeling.

Archangel faced the other man squarely. "If I may ask: how did you know about Kenzie? How did you know those implants were in his head? In fact, how did you recognize him?"

"While I was a 'guest' of the Legion, I happened to see his file in the lab."

"A file? What sort of file?"

"A file in von Brant's possession that had come from Malcolm Bullock's folio. It seems that your Mr. Graham was Bullock's only successful experiment. I assumed he must have died by now. Longevity was not a hallmark of Bullock's . . . subjects."

Archangel gazed off after the young Scotsman, who was chattering happily away with Ginny and some of the Resistance commandos. As he watched, Kenzie laughingly grasped Ginny by the shoulders and gave her a quick peck on the lips. Her reaction was not what Archangel expected. She did not slap Kenzie or pull away or burn his ears with scorn. Instead, the two of them simply gaped at each other as if the kiss had been a monumental surprise to both.

Archangel tried and failed to reconcile what he'd seen of the other products of Bullock's—and now von Brant's—experiments with his experience of Kenzie Graham.

"Let's keep this quiet for now," he told Tesla.

The scientist agreed immediately. "You have my word. I suspect the poor fellow has no idea what . . . what has been done to him."

Archangel knew that he'd been about to say "what he is." He wasn't sure any of them really understood that. What he'd seen of Iron Rail Jack had convinced him that the reanimates were soulless beings. Anyone who ever spent more than thirty seconds in MacKenzie Graham's presence knew he was anything but soulless.

"We'd best return to London," he told Tesla, and the two men moved to rejoin the assemblage of Resistance fighters and Paladins, which had grown as others rendezvoused in the woods.

"Well, gentlemen," Florian Buckingham hailed them as they approached. "I would say that was a rather successful operation."

"It was but one battle, Brigadier, not the war," Archangel told him. "However, Cross has suffered a rather sizable setback today, due largely to you and your men. I can't say we would've made it out of there if you hadn't shown up when you did." He hesitated then added, "The Resistance could certainly use your abilities as a field commander, and I would be proud to fight alongside you any day. May I hope that you will not return to your solitude?"

"Go back into hiding, you mean," said the brigadier. "Today has taught me that I would rather die a meaningful death than live a meaningless life." He extended his hand to Archangel. "May I hope that you will offer me a renewal of friendship as well as a field commission?"

Gratified, Archangel took the proffered hand in a firm clasp. "You may be assured of both."

It struck him as the surviving Resistance fighters made their way cross-country back to their vehicles, that he had not felt quite so whole in a very long time. Every man's heart drummed its final cadence alone. A man's or woman's last breath was shared only with God. He knew that. But just now, he was alive and not alone. To walk side by side with Florian Buckingham once more in duty and friendship had returned a part of Brenden Winter's soul that he had expected never to regain.

EPILOGUE

LONDON - ST. PANCRAS

THE UNDERGROUND RESISTANCE FACILITY WAS DESERTED EXCEPT BY one man, and dark but for the pool of warm golden light near the desk where he sat, recording his account of the battle at Enfield on a wax cylinder. Having finished with his recounting of the battle itself, he let his musings take him to the aftermath—to the rebirth of his friendship with Florian Buckingham.

He started the cylinder moving again and spoke once more into the speaking tube.

"We all die alone," he told the machine. "But if what we do in life catches fire in the blood of others and causes them to believe in something larger than their selves, then our actions, our essence, our spirit, will be immortalized by the storytellers. Our actions will live beyond us. In such a way, does a man achieve immortality. He lives on in the lives of those who have arisen to follow him.

"Archangel is more than a man. It is a symbol and a spirit of resistance and resilience. You who follow that spirit are angels and legend-makers. And so are the many who will arise after us, carrying on our cause and our spirit. Individuals may be stopped, as many have been since the Legion gained ascendance. But our crusade will not stop until evil has been crushed and we can all live as free beings, forever."

Winter turned off the machine, lifted the needle, and slid the cylinder from the spindle to lay it in the padded case that held an even dozen of his audio logs. On these devices, he had recorded everything from the last days of Victoria's reign to this moment. He closed the lid of the case and returned it to a desk drawer, then swivelled his chair to look up toward the softly lit alcove on the raised gallery at the far end of the room. He smiled a little, remembering Kenzie's musings about scientists and their labs. Within the alcove, illumined by a shaft of light, was the new Mark III armor Artemus and Bobby had designed and built for him. Lighter, stronger, with an improved set of weaponry.

It was a strange thing, Winter thought, that no matter what the circumstance, he seemed destined to serve *incognito*, whether it was through a secret life or a secret persona. He had served openly at the pleasure of the Crown, but what he did for the Crown remained, for the most part, hidden from sight. Now, his entire life was sub rosa. He was a ghost, a no-man, a legend that had no flesh on its bones. Anonymous. Invisible.

He swung back toward his desk, gaze falling on the portrait of Emily and Jon he kept atop it. The sepia print was static, flat, not even hinting at the vibrant auburn of Emily's hair, or the fresh cream of her skin or the warmth of her gaze. But it now called to mind the moment when he'd beheld them framed in a pane of glass in the bookstore entry. The memory was so painful, so raw, it forced Winter out of his chair and halfway across the lab—as if he could leave the pain behind him at his desk. As if he could outrun it, trick it, build a barricade against it.

He looked up at the Archangel armor again. Was that what the armor was? An attempt to evade, to block, to trick memory?

He tried to reason with the raw emotion within him. *I am doing this for them*, he told it. *This is how I keep them safe.*

Are they safe?

He had no real way of knowing that beyond having Kenzie or Ginny or Bobby occasionally gather news of them. He could not, given the situation, keep tabs on them himself or assign Resistance guards to them. Among the Resistance operatives only a handful knew that Archangel was a man who was presumed to have died in the commission of the most heinous act of regicide.

Not half an hour ago, Artemus had invited him to put on his Atkinson "skin" and join them for a well-deserved drink. Winter had pleaded that he needed to commit his report to wax before time dimmed his memory, and that he didn't feel like going out in any event. Now, suddenly, he felt very much like going out.

He checked the time. It was just coming on six o'clock. It being Sunday, the evening service at St. Giles-in-the-Fields would be commencing in an hour's time. He knew that as well as he knew the rising and setting of the Sun. Memory assailed him, again: standing on the steps of St. Giles with his wife and son, laughing over a hat worn by one of the wealthy parishioners that had blocked their view of the entire choir. How many times had they lingered in the churchyard, welcoming the first fall of snow or the first drift of falling spring blossoms or admiring the winking lights of a skyship passing by overhead?

He hardly knew he had moved when he found himself at his desk again, applying his Atkinson disguise with practiced hands. If those hands trembled just a bit, he pretended not to notice. He was simply doing reconnaissance, making sure his family was safe and sound. That was all.

He was at the church with sufficient time to loiter about the front steps as the parishioners arrived. Time passed; more and more people entered the church, but there was still no sign of Emily and Jon. He fretted. He became worried that his loss had caused them to change their habit, or even lose their faith. So, when they arrived at last on foot, walking briskly, he was elated.

He made himself look away from them, aware that a strange man staring at them could be nothing but alarming. He tracked them in his peripheral vision and followed them into the sanctuary. He was at once swathed in warmth and light and the scent of candle wax, and stopped to breathe it in as Emily and Jonathan found seats in the pews.

They sat where the family had always sat for worship, toward the front of the congregation in the right hand section and close to the central aisle. He seated himself in an upper level gallery from which he could see them clearly. Or at least, he could see Jon clearly. Emily was wearing a bonnet with a black feather on it that obscured half of her face. Jon's face was obscured in a different way; the boy he had been was being over-written by the man he was becoming. When he rose to sing hymns, he stood nearly as tall as his mother.

Winter hadn't noticed that at the bookstore. He'd been too concerned with concealing himself. Now, he indulged his heart and kept his eyes on his family as the priest sermonized and the choir sang and the congregation joined in the call and response of prayer. He sat through the entire service, barely registering what was said or sung. He stood and sat with the rest of the worshippers, opened his mouth and closed his eyes and murmured prayers, but his eyes were for his wife and child, alone.

When it was over, he descended the stairs to the front gate quickly, hoping to catch sight of them as they left the church. Standing off to the side of the entrance near the stone arch that gave onto the street, he waited until they stepped out into the light of the electric lamps in the church yard. They were both silent as they moved toward him, Jon looking older than his twelve years, and a bit stern, Emily gazing up toward the sky with a dreamy look on her face.

What are you thinking? What do you feel? Do you even remember me?

A stupid question, he knew. The fact that she still dressed herself in dove grey and black spoke volumes about the state of her heart—a heart he had broken.

No, a heart the Legion had broken.

She glanced aside as she neared the church's gate and, for just a second, their eyes met. He all but fell to his knees on the spot, but somehow remained upright, doffed his hat and murmured, "Good evening."

She smiled gently and nodded in reply, but on the point of exiting the gate, she spared him a second glance, her brow slightly furrowed as if . . . .

Then, they were walking away from him, arm in arm, toward their home, and he fought his wiser self to follow them. His wiser self lost that battle. He trailed them at a distance all the way to the house, then stood in the shadows of an aging fir for some time, watching lights go on and off within the Winter household, imagining his wife and son at supper, and wishing with all his heart that he could put himself in that empty chair across from Emily at the dining table.

Did she look at it often? Did she imagine him sitting there?

Perhaps it was the cold, or the pain of loss, or the final victory of reason over emotion, but after above half an hour of torturing himself, Brenden Winter finally slipped away into the darkness and sought a cab back to St. Pancras.

LONDON - NEAR TOWER BRIDGE

Viktor von Brant felt as if his skin wanted to crawl from his body as he navigated the narrow, oppressive lanes near the Thames just above the Tower Bridge. If he could have levitated himself above the mud-slick cobbles and the squalid contents of the gutters, he would have. Lacking that ability, he simply hunched his shoulders, pulled his muffler up over his nose to keep out the dreadful smell, and soldiered on.

He stopped beneath the wan, fitful light of a streetlamp to check the paper in his hand once more, squinting at the worn addresses on the anonymous buildings. Slightly reassured, he turned right, into an even narrower alley. As he approached the building he assumed the directions indicated, a hand snaked out of the darkness and yanked him into a doorway. His breath left his lungs in a rush and he wheezed and bleated in terror.

"So good of you to come, Doctor," said the man whose hand still lay heavily on his shoulder.

"Captain Judd," Viktor gasped when he'd recovered a bit of his wind, "you have developed a most disconcerting habit. Could you not have chosen a safer place to meet?"

Judd chuckled—a low, almost purring sound that reminded Viktor of a panther he had seen at the London Zoo.

"You're completely safe here. How could you not be? You're among friends."

"Friends!" repeated the scientist. "I would not call us friends."

Judd clicked his tongue in mild rebuke. "Not friends? After I went and saved your life and all?"

Viktor swallowed his exasperation, knowing he was cornered. He still managed a bit of asperity. "So, what is it? What is so important that you must drag me out here on this cold, damp evening?"

Judd poked his head out of the alcove and peered up and down the alley before reaching into the pocket of his coat and presenting his frightened companion with a small wooden box.

No, thought Viktor. *It cannot be . . . .*

He took the box in quaking hands and opened it. It was Pandora's box, surely, exuding awe, confusion, and a myriad questions. He looked up into the skyraider's dark, handsome face.

"I . . . I don't understand. How did you get these? I thought the Ether units were all destroyed."

Judd favored him with a lopsided grin. "Apparently not."

"Does Cross know about these?"

The grin vanished, leaving no doubt about the pirate's intent. "No. And he never will. These—" He tapped the edge of the box with the tip of a finger. "—will be our little secret, Herr Doktor."

"Our . . . I don't understand. You will not tell Mr. Cross?"

"I am having some equipment set up for you in a new and secret location." Judd gave Viktor's shoulder a gentle shake. "Together, Doctor, we will make history."

Judd reached up and snapped the box shut, nearly pinching the reverent tips of the scientist's fingers. He then snatched the box back and tucked it away out of sight.

"How?" asked Viktor, trying not to let his mingled excitement and dread manifest in a case of the shivers. "What do you want me to do?"

"Stay put for now and pay attention to what's going on around you. If you keep your eyes and ears sharp for what Cross is planning, it will be of great service to me . . . and trust me when I say it is in your best interests to be of service to Mordecai Judd. I'll be in touch shortly. Good evening, Herr Doktor." Judd touched his fingertips to the brim of his hat, peered out of the doorway, then slipped into the gathering mist and disappeared.

Viktor von Brant stayed behind for a moment, leaning against the grimy bricks. He forced himself to breathe, to hold his urge to shiver and shake at bay. Finally, with a deep breath, he dove into the mist like a swimmer into treacherous waters.

Judd had completely disappeared by the time Viktor approached the intersection where the alley met the narrow street. He would catch the first hansom cab he saw and have it carry him home to his warm fire and a pot of tea. Yes, that was exactly what he'd do.

The sound of jingling metal from low on the wall in front of him caused him to lose his newly won composure. He yelped and leapt aside, away from the sound. An old beggar in a ragged brown coat hunkered against the wall of the building to his left, rattling coins in a metal cup.

"Pardon, guv'ner," the wretch said, peering up from beneath the brim of a filthy bowler. "Might ye have a penny or two for a sick old man?"

"Nein! No! I have no coins. That is, I need them for cab fare. I'm sorry. I'm *sorry!*"

Viktor pulled his muffler up over his nose again and all but ran toward the nearest streetlamp. He looked back twice at the vagrant, fearful that the aged beggar might be following him. The first time, the creature was watching him with a strange smile playing about his toothless mouth.

The second time, he was gone.

ABOUT THE AUTHOR

A NEW YORK TIMES BESTSELLING AUTHOR, MAYA BECAME addicted to science fiction as the result of a hair-raising encounter with a robot named Gort. Her dad let her stay up late to watch "The Day the Earth Stood Still" when she was 6 and Maya was never the same.

Her debut novel, "The Meri" (Baen), was a Locus Magazine 1992 Best First Novel nominee (now available as a trade paperback from Sense of Wonder Press). Since, she has published eight more speculative fiction novels, including "Mr. Twilight" (with Michael Reaves) and also worked with Michael on "Star Wars - Coruscant Nights III: Patterns of Force", "Star Wars: Shadow Games" and the New York Times Bestseller and Science Fiction Club selection, "THE LAST JEDI" –fourth book in the Coruscant Nights series.

She recently stepped sideways into the world of mystery/crime novels with her first Gina Miyoko mystery—THE ANTIQUITIES HUNTER. "I've read mysteries all my life and I love them. I realize I've embedded a mystery of some sort in almost everything I've written. I'm thrilled that I'm finally working in the genre."

ABOUT THE SCREENWRITER

Dave Di Pietro has over 38 years' experience within the film and video industries. Beginning by shooting Super-8 movies while still in high school, it wasn't long before he joined a group of fellow filmmakers and formed Cinema Group 4, a small film society.

While at the New Jersey based organization, he began writing and directing, as well as producing special effects for their in-house films. Their grandest accomplishment was a 16mm feature based on Arthur C. Clarke's novel Rendezvous with Rama.

Dave eventually went to work for Paramount Pictures for over 13 years. While there, he wrote and directed a pilot for the SyFy Channel called, Quad 9, which was about a space station at the edge of our galaxy, set up to patrol and police this dangerous frontier.

He is now writing and directing for both stage and screen in the Atlanta, Georgia area, which is becoming the Hollywood of the East. He has formed Reel Cool Entertainment, which is an independent, full-service production company. Their focus is creating original intellectual property and online content for the international film, television and video game markets.

Make sure to follow us on social media
to stay informed about the Archangel film,
as well as all of our other upcoming projects!

www.ReelCoolEntertainment.com
www.facebook.com/archangeltheseries
www.instagram.com/archangel1893

CPSIA information can be obtained
at www.ICGtesting.com
Printed in the USA
FFHW020928110519
52388429-57796FF